BUYING A FISHING ROD FOR MY GRANDFATHER

BUYING A FISHING ROD
FOR MY GRANDFATHER

GAO XINGJIAN

Translated from the Chinese by Mabel Lee

RETIRÉ DE LA COLLECTION UNIVERSELLE

Bibliothèque et Archives nationales du Québec

HarperCollins*Publishers*

An extension of this copyright page appears on page 127.

FIRST EDITION

Printed on acid-free paper

Library of Congress Cataloging-in-Publication Data

Gao, Xingjian.
   [Gei wo lao ye mai yu gan. English]
   Buying a fishing rod for my grandfather: stories / Gao Xingjian; [translated by Mabel Lee].—1st ed.
      p.   cm.
   Contents: The temple—In the park—Cramp—The accident—Buying a fishing rod for my grandfather—In an instant.
   ISBN 0-06-057555-7
   I. Title.
PL2869.O128G4513   2004
895.1'352—dc21

                                        2003051138

04 05 06 07 08   ❖/RRD   10 9 8 7 6 5 4 3 2 1

CONTENTS

BUYING A FISHING ROD
FOR MY GRANDFATHER

THE TEMPLE

We were deliriously happy: delirious with the hope, infatuation, tenderness, and warmth that go with a honeymoon. Fangfang and I had planned the trip over and over, even though we had only half a month off: ten days of wedding leave, plus one week of additional work leave. Getting married is a major event in life, and for us nothing was more important, so why not ask for some extra time? That director of mine was so miserly: anyone who went to him requesting leave had to haggle; there were never instant approvals. The two weeks I had written in my application he changed to one week, including a Sunday, and it was with reluctance that he said, "I'll expect you to be back at work by the due date."

"Of course, of course," I said. "We wouldn't be able to afford the salary deduction if we stayed any longer." It was only then that he signed his name, thereby granting us permission to go on leave.

I wasn't a bachelor anymore. I had a family. I would no longer be able to go off to restaurants with friends as soon as I got paid at the beginning of the month. I wouldn't be able to spend so recklessly that by the end of the month I wouldn't have the money to buy a pack of cigarettes and would have to go through my pockets and search the drawers for coins. But I won't go into all that. I'm saying that I—we—were very happy. In our short lives, there hadn't been much happiness. Both Fangfang and I had experienced years of hardship, and we had learned what life was all about. During those catastrophic years in this country, our families suffered through many misfortunes, and to some extent we still resented our generation's fate. But I won't go into that, either. What was important was that we could now count ourselves happy.

We had half a month's leave, and although it was only half a honeymoon, for us it couldn't have been sweeter. I am not going to go into how sweet it was. You all know about that and have experienced it yourselves, but this particular sweetness was ours alone. What I want to tell you about is the Temple of Perfect Benevolence: "perfect" as in "perfect union," and "benevolence" as in "benevolent love." But the name of the temple is not really of great importance. It was a dilapidated ruin, and certainly not a famous tourist attraction. No one knew about it other than the locals, and I suspect that even the locals who knew what it was called were few. In any case, the temple we happened to visit wasn't one where people burned incense or prayed, and if we hadn't carefully examined the stone tablet with traces of writing in the drain of the water pump we wouldn't even have known that the temple had a name. The locals referred to it as "the big temple," but it was nothing compared with the Retreat for the Soul Temple, in Hangzhou, or the Jade Cloud Temple, in Beijing. Situated on a hill beyond the town, it was little more than an old two-story building with flying eaves and the remnants of a stone gate in front of it. The courtyard walls had collapsed. The bricks of the outer wall had been carried off by peasants to build their houses or construct pens for their pigs, and only a circle of unfired bricks remained, overgrown with weeds.

However, from a distance, from the small street of the county town, the glazed yellow tiles sparkling in the sunlight caught our eyes. We had come to this town quite by accident. Our train was still at the platform after the announced departure time, probably waiting for an express that was behind schedule to pass through. The chaotic scramble of passengers getting on and off had settled and, apart from the conductors chatting at the carriage doors, there was no one on the platform. Beyond the station was a valley with an expanse of gray roofs. Farther still, a chain of heavily wooded mountains gave this ancient town an exceptional air of tranquillity.

Suddenly I had an idea. I said, "Should we take a look at this town?"

Fangfang, sitting opposite and looking at me lovingly, gave a slight nod. Her eyes seemed to speak, and, sensitive to each other, we communicated on the same wavelength. Without a word, we took our bags from the luggage rack

5

and rushed to the door of our carriage. As soon as we had jumped onto the platform, we both laughed.

I said, "We'll leave on the next train."

"I don't mind if we don't leave at all," Fangfang answered.

After all, we were traveling, and it was our honeymoon. If we fell in love with a place, we would go there, and if we went on liking the place, we would stay longer. All the time, wherever we went, the happiness of newlyweds accompanied us. We were the happiest people in the world. Fangfang was holding my arm; I was holding our bags. We wanted the conductors on the platform and the countless pairs of eyes on the other side of the train windows to look at us with envy.

We no longer had to drive ourselves mad trying to get transferred back to the city. Nor did we have to keep begging our parents for help. And we didn't have to worry about our residential status or our jobs anymore. We even had our own apartment, our own home; it wasn't very big, but it was comfortable. You belonged to me and I belonged to you, and, Fangfang, I know what you want to say: *Our relationship was no longer immoral!* And what does that mean? It means that we want everyone to share in our happiness. We've had so many problems, and we've troubled all of you with them, and you have all worried because of us. How can we repay you? With some candies and cigarettes after our wedding? No, we are repaying you with our happiness. There's nothing wrong with what I'm saying, is there?

That was how we came to this quiet old town in the valley. But it turned out that the town was nowhere near as tranquil as it had seemed when we were looking out the train window. Below the gray roof tiles, the lanes and alleys throbbed with activity. It was nine in the morning, and people were selling vegetables, rock melons, and freshly picked apples and pears. Streets in county towns like this one aren't wide, so mule carts, horse carts, and trucks were all jammed together, with drivers cracking their whips and honking their horns. Dust filling the air, dirty water tossed out beside vegetable stalls, melon rinds all over the ground, squawking hens flapping in the hands of their buyers: these were sights that made us feel close to the town.

It all felt so different from the time when we were graduates sent to work in the countryside. Now we were just visitors passing through, tourists, and the complicated relationships between the people here had nothing to do with us. Inevitably, this made us city dwellers feel somewhat superior. Fangfang clutched my arm tightly and I leaned close to her, and we could sense people's eyes on us. But we didn't belong to this town; we were from another world. We walked right past them, but they didn't gossip about us; they only gossiped about the people they knew.

Eventually, there were no more vegetable stalls and very few people. We had left behind the bustle and din of the market. I saw from my watch that it had taken us only a half hour to walk the length of the main road from the railway station. It was still early. It would be an anticlimax just to return to the station and wait for the next train, and Fangfang was already thinking about spending the night here!

She didn't say so, but I could see her disappointment. A man was heading toward us, ostentatiously swinging his arms as he walked. He was probably a cadre.

"Excuse me, could you tell me how to get to the county hostel?" I asked.

He looked at Fangfang and me for a moment, then enthusiastically pointed it out to us. "Go that way," he told us, "then head left. The red three-story brick building is the county hostel." He asked whom we were looking for, and seemed to want to take us there himself. We explained that we were tourists passing through and asked if there were any sights worth seeing. He patted his head: this, it seemed, was a problem.

After giving the matter some thought, he said, "There actually aren't any scenic spots in this county. But there's a big temple up on the hill to the west of town, if you want to go there. You'll have to climb the hill, though, and it's steep!"

"That's not a problem. We've come here to do some hiking," I said.

Fangfang hastened to add, "That's right. We're not afraid of climbing a hill."

8

At this, the man led us to the corner of the street. The hill was now directly in front, and at the top was the old temple, its glazed tiles sparkling in the sun.

But then the man glanced at the high-heeled shoes Fangfang was wearing and said, "You'll have to wade across a river."

"Is the water deep?" I asked.

"Above the knees."

I looked at Fangfang.

"That's nothing. I'll manage." She didn't want to let me down.

We thanked him and began walking in the direction he had indicated. When we turned onto the dusty dirt road, I couldn't help but feel bad as I looked at the new high-heeled shoes with thin straps that Fangfang had on. Still, she charged ahead.

"You're really a crazy little thing," I said, catching up with her.

"As long as I'm with you." Do you remember, Fangfang? You said this as you nestled against me.

We followed a path down to the riverbank. On both sides, corn grew straight, taller than a man, and we walked through the green gauze canopy, with no one in sight either ahead or behind. Taking Fangfang in my arms, I gently kissed her. What's wrong with that? She doesn't want me to talk about that. So let's go back to the Temple of Perfect Benevolence. It was on the other side of the river, at the top of the hill. We could see tufts of weeds growing between the glistening yellow tiles.

The river was clear and cool. I held Fangfang's shoes and my leather sandals in one hand and Fangfang's hand in the other, while she scooped up her skirt with her free hand. Barefoot, we felt our way across. It had been a long time since I'd walked barefoot, so my feet were sensitive to even the smooth stones on the riverbed.

"Is it hurting your feet?" I asked Fangfang.

"I like it," you replied softly. On our honeymoon, even having sore feet was a happy sensation. All the misfortunes of the world seemed to flow away with the river water, and we returned for a moment to our youth. We frolicked in the water like mischievous children.

As I steadied her with one hand, Fangfang leaped from rock to rock, and from time to time she hummed a song. Once across the river, we started to run up the hill, laughing and shouting. Then Fangfang cut her foot and I was very upset, but she comforted me, saying that it was all right, it would be nothing as soon as she put on her shoes. I said that it was my fault, but she replied that she'd do anything to make me happy, even let her feet get cut. All right, all right, I won't go on about it. But because you are the friends we value most, who have shared our anxieties with us, we should also share our happiness with you.

It was in this manner that we finally climbed to the top of the hill and arrived at the outer gate in front of the temple. Within the collapsed courtyard wall was a gutter with pure water from the pump running through. In what had been the courtyard, someone had planted a patch of vegetables, and next to that was a manure pit. We recalled the years we had spent shoveling manure with production units in the countryside. Those difficult times had trickled away like water, leaving some sadness but sweet memories as well. And there was our love, too. In the glorious sunlight, no one could interfere with this secure love of ours. No one would be able to harm us again.

Near the big temple was an iron incense burner. It was probably too heavy to move and too thick to break apart, so it continued to keep the old temple company, standing guard in front of the main door. The door was padlocked. Boards had been nailed over the rotten wooden lattice windows, but they, too, had rotted. The place was probably now being used as a storehouse for the local production team.

No one else was around, and it was very peaceful. We could hear the mountain wind moaning in the ancient pines in front of the temple, and as no one was there to disturb us, we lay down on the grass in the shade of the trees. Fang-fang rested her head on my arm, and we looked up at a thread of cloud about to disappear into the blue sky. Ours was an indescribable happiness, a true contentment.

Intoxicated by this tranquillity, we would have gone on lying there, but we heard heavy footsteps on the flagstones.

Fangfang sat up, and I got to my feet to have a look. A man was walking along the stone path from the gate toward the temple. He was a big fellow, with a mass of tangled hair on his head and an untrimmed beard covering his cheeks. He was scowling. From beneath bushy eyebrows, his stern eyes surveyed us. The wind had turned cool. Probably noticing our curious looks, the man raised his head slightly in the direction of the temple. Then, squinting, he studied the weeds swaying among the shiny tiles.

He stopped in front of the incense burner and, striking it with one hand, made it ring. His fingers, gnarled and rough, looked as if they, too, were made of cast iron. In his other hand he held a tattered black cotton bag. He didn't seem to be a commune member who had come to tend the vegetables. He was sizing us up again, looking at Fangfang's high-heeled shoes and our travel bags in the grass. Fangfang immediately put her shoes back on. Then, unexpectedly, he addressed us.

"Are you from out of town? Are you enjoying yourselves here?"

I nodded.

"It's good weather," he said. He seemed to want to talk.

The eyes under those thick eyebrows had become less stern, and he appeared well meaning. He was wearing leather shoes with soles made from rubber tires, and the seams had split in places. The legs of his trousers were wet, so it was obvious he had come across the river from town.

"It's cool, and the view is quite beautiful," I said.

"Sit down. I'll be leaving shortly."

It seemed that he was offering a kind of apology. He, too, sat down on the grass beside the flagstones.

He opened his bag and said, "Would you like a melon?"

"No, thanks," I immediately said. But he threw me one anyway. I caught it and was about to throw it back.

"It's nothing. I've got half a bag of them here," he said, raising the heavy bag to show me and taking out another melon as he spoke. I couldn't say no, so I took a parcel of snacks from my travel bag, opened it, and held it out to him. "Try our snacks," I said.

He took a small piece of cake and put it on top of his bag.

"That's enough for me," he said. "Go on, eat it." He squeezed the melon in his big hands, cracking the brittle skin. "They're clean. I washed them in the river." He tossed away a piece of rind and shouted in the direction of the gate, "Take a break! Come and eat some melon!"

"But there are long-horned grasshoppers here!" A boy's voice came from beyond the gate; then the boy himself appeared on the slope, holding a wire cage.

"There are plenty of them. I'll catch some for you later," the man replied.

The little boy came toward us, bouncing and jumping as he ran.

"Is it school vacation?" I asked, and, copying the man, cracked our melon into pieces.

"It's Sunday today, so I brought him out," he replied.

We were so engrossed with our own holiday that we had forgotten what day of the week it was. Fangfang took a bite of the melon and smiled at me to indicate that he was a good man. There are, in fact, many good people in the world.

"Eat it. It's from Uncle and Auntie over there," he said to the boy, who was staring at the cream cake on top of his bag. The boy had grown up in this town and had clearly never seen such a cake. He took it and ate it right away.

"Is he your son?" I asked.

The man didn't reply, but said to the boy, "Take some melon and go play. I'll catch grasshoppers for you later."

"I want to catch five of them!" the boy said.

"All right, we'll catch five."

The man watched as the boy ran off with the wire cage in his hand. There were deep creases at the corners of his eyes.

"He isn't my son," he said, looking down and taking out a cigarette. He struck a match and dragged hard. Then, sensing our surprise, he added, "He's the child of my paternal cousin. I want to adopt him, but it depends on whether he's willing to come and stay with me."

Suddenly we understood that this stern man's heart was churning with emotion.

"What about your wife?" Fangfang couldn't help asking. There was no reply. He puffed hard on his cigarette, got up, and left.

We felt the chill of the mountain air. On the brilliant yellow tiles, the fresh grass that had sprouted in the spring was as tall as the old, withered stalks, and both swayed in the breeze. In the blue sky, a floating cloud that seemed to hang on the corner of a flying eave created the impression that the temple itself was tilting. A broken tile at the edge of the eave looked as if it were about to fall. Probably it had sat that way for years without falling.

The man was standing on a mound that had once been a wall, and for a long time he just stared out at the mountains and valleys. In the distance the ridges were higher and steeper than the hill we were on, but on the mountain slopes there were no terraced fields and no houses to be seen.

"You shouldn't have asked him," I said.

"Oh stop." Fangfang looked upset.

"There's a grasshopper here!" came the boy's voice from the other side of the hill. It seemed far away but was quite clear.

The man strode off in that direction, swinging the bag of rock melons as he disappeared from sight. I put a hand on Fangfang's shoulder and pulled her toward me.

"Don't." She turned away.

"There's a bit of grass in your hair," I explained, removing a pine needle that had stuck to her hair.

"That tile is about to fall," Fangfang said. She, too, had noticed the broken tile hanging there precariously. "It would be good if it fell. Otherwise it might injure someone," she mumbled.

"It might be a while before it does fall," I said.

We walked to the mound where the man had been standing. In the valley there was a stretch of farmland, dense crops of luxuriant green barley and broomcorn millet, waiting for the autumn harvest. Below us, on a level part of the slope, stood a few mud huts, their bottom halves newly coated in brilliant white lime. The man was holding the boy's hand as they made their way down a small winding track, past the huts and through the crops. Suddenly, like a colt that had broken free of its reins, the boy bolted off, dashing ahead, then turning and running back. He seemed to be waving the cage at the man.

"Do you think the man caught grasshoppers for him?" Fangfang, do you remember asking me that?

"Of course," I said. "Of course."

"He caught five of them!" you said cheekily.

Well, that's the Temple of Perfect Benevolence that we visited on our honeymoon, and which I wanted to describe for all of you.

IN THE PARK

"I haven't strolled in a park for a long time. I never have the time to spare, or the inclination anymore."

"It's the same with everyone. After work, people just hurry home. Life's always a rush."

"I remember when I was a child, I really liked coming to this park to roll around on the grass."

"I used to come with my father and mother."

"I really liked it when there were other children."

"Yes."

"Especially when you were there as well."

"I remember."

"At the time, you had two little plaits."

"At the time, you always wore dungarees, and you were very cocky."

"You were unfriendly, always haughty."

"Really?"

"Yes, nobody would dare antagonize you."

"I don't remember, but I liked playing with you and I even used to kick a rubber ball with you."

"Nonsense, you didn't ever kick a rubber ball! You used to wear little white shoes and were always afraid of getting them dirty."

"That's right, when I was little I was really fond of wearing white sneakers."

"You were like a princess."

"Sure—a princess wearing sneakers."

"Then your family moved."

"That's right."

"At first you often came to visit on Sundays, but later on not as much."

"I had grown up."

"My mother really liked you."

"I know."

"There were no daughters in our family."

"Everyone said we looked alike, like an older sister and a younger brother."

"Don't forget we're the same age, that I'm two months older."

"But I seemed older than you; I was always taller by a hand, as if I were your older sister."

"At the time, girls got tall earlier. Enough of that, let's talk about something else."

"What will we talk about, then?"

The path under the trees has clipped Japan cypresses growing on both sides. On the slope behind the cypresses, a young woman wearing a dress and carrying a red handbag sits down on a stone bench.

"Let's sit down awhile, too."

"All right."

20

"The sun's about to set."

"Yes, it's beautiful."

"I don't like this artificial sort of beauty."

"Didn't you say you liked going to parks?"

"That was when I was little. I've lived in the mountain regions. I was a woodcutter for seven years in primitive forests."

"You managed to survive."

"Forests are really awesome."

The young woman wearing a dress gets up from the stone bench and looks to the end of the shady path beyond the neatly clipped cypresses. Several people are coming from that direction, among them a tall youth with hair over his temples. Beyond the treetops and the wall, the sky is infused with brilliant red and purple-red colors of the sunset, and rippling clouds begin to spread overhead.

"I haven't seen a beautiful sunset like this for a long time. The sky seems to be on fire."

"It's like a wildfire."

"Like what?"

"It's like a forest wildfire . . ."

"Well, keep talking."

"When there's a forest wildfire, the sky is just like this. The fire spreads swiftly and with a vengeance, and there's not time to cut down the forest. It's really terrifying. All the felled trees fly into the air, and from a distance they look like bits of straw drifting up in a fire, and crazed leopards come out of the forests to throw themselves into the rivers, swimming right at you—"

"Don't the leopards attack people?"

"They're past thinking about that."

"Can't you use your rifles on them?"

"People are also traumatized; from riverbanks they just stare vacantly at the fire."

"Isn't there anything that can be done?"

"Mountain streams can't stop it. The trees on the other side get scorched, start crackling, and suddenly they're alight. For a distance of more than several *li* around it's so smoky and hot, you can't breathe. All you can do is wait for the wind to change or for the fire to get to the river, exhaust itself, and burn out."

The young woman in the dress sits down again on the stone bench; her red handbag is beside her.

"Tell me some more about your experiences during those years."

"There's nothing much to tell."

"How can there be nothing much to tell? All that was very interesting."

"But there's not much point in talking about all that now. Talk about what *you've* been doing all these years."

"Me?"

"Yes, you."

"I've got a daughter."

"How old?"

"Six."

"Is she just like you?"

"Everyone says she's just like me."

"Is she like you when you were little? Does she wear white sneakers?"

"No, she likes to wear leather shoes. Her father buys her one pair after another."

"You're lucky. He sounds like a nice person."

"He's quite good to me, but I don't know if I'm lucky or not."

"And isn't your work also quite good?"

"Yes, compared with what many other people my age do, my work's all right. I sit in an office, answer the phone, and take documents to my superiors."

"Are you a secretary?"

"I'm looking after documents."

"That sort of work is confidential, it shows that they trust you."

"It's much better than being a laborer. Didn't you also manage to get through a hard time? Since you went to university, I suppose you're doing some kind of professional work now?"

"Yes, but it was all through my own efforts."

The colors of the sunset vanish. The sky is now a dark red, but on the horizon, above the treetops, there is an orange-yellow glow on the edge of a dark cloud. On the slope it is becoming dark in the grove and the young woman on the bench is sitting with her head bowed. She seems to look at her watch and then stands up. She is holding her handbag but decides to put it down again on the bench, as she looks at the path beyond the cypresses. Apparently noticing the moon by the clouds, she turns away and starts to pace, her eyes looking at the ground.

"She's waiting for someone."

"Waiting for someone is awful. Nowadays it's the young men who don't show up for dates."

"Are there too many young women in the city?"

"There's no shortage of young men, it's just that there are too few decent young men."

"But this young woman is very good looking."

"If the woman falls in love first, it's always unlucky."

"Will he turn up?"

"Who knows? Having to wait really makes a person go crazy."

"Luckily we're past that age. Have you ever waited for someone?"

"It was he who first sought me. Have you ever made someone wait?"

"I've never failed to show up for a date."

"Do you have a girlfriend?"

"I seem to."

"Then why don't you get married?"

"I probably will."

"It seems you don't really like her."

"I feel sorry for her."

"Feeling sorry is not love. If you don't love her, don't go on deceiving her!"

"I've only ever deceived myself."

"That's also deceiving the other person."

"Let's talk about something else."

"All right."

The young woman sits down. Then she immediately stands up again, looking toward the path. The last smudge of faint red on the horizon is barely visible. She sits down again but, as if sensing people are watching, she puts down her head and appears to be fiddling with her skirt at the knees.

"Will he turn up?"

"I don't know."

"This shouldn't happen."

"There are too many things that shouldn't happen."

"Is this girlfriend of yours pretty?"

"She is a sad case."

"Don't talk like that! If you don't love her, don't deceive her. Just find yourself a young woman you truly love, someone good-looking."

"Someone good-looking wouldn't necessarily like me."

"Why?"

"Because I don't have a good father."

"Don't talk like that, I don't want to listen."

"Then it's best not to listen. I think we should leave."

"Will you come to my home?"

"I should bring your daughter a present. It will also count as my best wishes to you."

"Don't talk like that."

"What's wrong with that?"

"You're always hurting me."

"That's never been my intention."

"I wish you happiness."

"I don't want to hear that word."

"Then aren't you happy?"

"I don't want to talk about it. It's been hard just to meet this once after all these years, so let's not talk about depressing things like that."

"Very well, then let's talk about something else."

The young woman suddenly stands up. Someone is coming along the path, walking very quickly.

"Well, at least he's turned up."

It's a youth carrying a canvas satchel. He doesn't slow down and keeps walking. The young woman looks away.

"It's not the person she's waiting for. Life's often that way, oddly enough."

"She's crying."

"Who?"

The young woman sits down with her hands over her face, her hands are raised and seem to be covering her face, but it can't be seen clearly. Birds are twittering.

"So there are still birds here."

"Not only forests have birds."

"Well, there are still sparrows here."

"You've become quite arrogant."

"That's how I managed to survive. If I hadn't kept that bit of arrogance, I wouldn't be here today."

"Don't be so cynical; you're not the only person who has suffered. Everyone was sent to work in the country. You should realize that it was much worse for the young women sent to the country where they had neither relatives or friends. The reason I married him was because I had no better option. His parents arranged for my transfer back to the city."

"I wasn't blaming you."

"No one has the right to blame anyone."

The streetlights have turned on and produce a wan yellow light among the green leaves of the trees. The night sky is gray and indistinct; even the stars can't be seen clearly in the city sky, making the light from the streetlights among the trees appear too bright.

"I think we should leave."

"Yes, we shouldn't have come here."

"People might think we are lovers. If your husband finds out, he won't misunderstand, will he?"

"He's not that kind of person."

"Then, he's a pretty good person."

"You can come and stay at our place."

"Only if he invites me."

"Won't it be the same if I invite you?"

"Too bad I didn't know your address. That was why I went to look you up at your workplace. Otherwise, I would have gone directly to visit you at home."

"You don't have to go into all that nonsense."

"There's no need for us to snipe at each other like that."

"You're the one who is saying one thing and meaning something else."

"Let's talk about something else."

"All right."

It has become dark in the grove and the young woman can no longer be seen. However, with the light shining on them, the lustrous green leaves of a white poplar seem to glow. There's a hint of a breeze, and the trembling leaves of the white poplar shimmer like satin.

"She hasn't left yet, has she?"

"No, she's leaning against a tree."

A big tree stands a few paces from the empty stone bench, and someone is leaning against it.

"What's she doing?"

"Crying."

"It's not worth it!"

"Why not?"

"It's not worth crying over him. She won't have a problem finding a good man who loves her, a person worthy of her love. She should just leave."

"But she's still hoping."

"Life's road is wide and she will find her own way."

"Don't think you know everything; you don't understand how a woman feels. It's just so easy for a man to hurt a woman. The woman is always weaker."

"If she knows she is weaker, why doesn't she try to learn to be stronger?"

"Fine-sounding words."

"There's no need to look for things to worry about. There are enough worries in life. One should be able to accept things."

"There are so many things that should be."

"I'm saying that people should only do the things that they should do."

"That's the same as saying nothing."

"Quite right. I shouldn't have come to see you."

"That's also saying nothing."

"All right, we should go. I'll buy you dinner."

"I don't want to eat. Can't we talk about something else?"

"What about?"

"Talk about yourself."

"Let's talk about the next generation. What's your daughter's name?"

"I wanted to have a son."

"Having a daughter is the same."

"No. When a boy grows up he won't have to suffer as much."

"People of the future won't have as much suffering, because we've already suffered for them."

"She's crying."

The sound of rustling leaves is in the breeze overhead, but the sound of weeping is clearly in it, and coming from the direction of the stone bench and the tree.

"We should go and console her."

"It wouldn't help."

"But we should still try."

"Then *you* go."

"In such a situation it would only be appropriate for a woman to go."

"She doesn't need that sort of consolation."

"I don't understand."

"You don't understand anything."

"Best not to. Once you do, it becomes a burden."

"Then why do you want to console others? Why don't you just console yourself?"

"What do you mean?"

"You don't understand how other people feel. If feelings are a burden, it's best for you not to understand."

"Let's leave."

"Will you come to my home?"

"There's no need."

"Are we going to say good-bye just like that? I've already invited you to come for dinner tomorrow. He'll be there, too."

"I think it would be best if I didn't come. What do you think?"

"That's entirely up to you."

In the darkness, the sound of weeping becomes more distinct. Intermittently, stifled sobs mingle with the sound of leaves trembling in the evening breeze.

"When I get married I'll write you a letter."

"It's best that you don't write anything."

"If I pass through for work later on, I might come to visit you again."

"It's best that you don't."

"Yes, it was a mistake."

"What mistake are you talking about?"

"I shouldn't have come to see you again."

"No, it wasn't a mistake for you to have come!"

"Neither of us is to blame. The mistakes of that era are to blame. But all that's in the past and we have to learn to forget."

"But it's hard to forget everything."

"Maybe with the passing of more time . . ."

"You had best go."

"Don't you want me to see you onto a bus?"

The two of them stand up. From behind the gray tree trunk near the barely visible empty stone bench, there is a sob that couldn't be stifled. However, the person can't be seen.

"Do you think maybe it'd be best that we urge her to go home?"

The silky, tender, new green leaves on the white poplar shimmer in the glow of the streetlight.

CRAMP

Cramp. His stomach is starting to cramp. Of course, he thought he could swim farther out. But about a kilometer from shore his stomach is starting to cramp. At first he thinks it's a stomachache—that will pass if he keeps moving. But when his stomach keeps tightening, he stops swimming any farther and feels it with his hand. The right side is hard, and he knows it's a cramp in his stomach because of the cold water. He hadn't exercised enough to prepare himself before entering the water. After dinner, he had set off alone from the little white hostel and had come to the beach. It was early autumn, windy, and at dusk, few people were going into the water. Everyone was either chatting or playing poker. In the middle of the day men and women were lying everywhere on the beach, but now there were only five or six people playing volleyball, a young woman in a red swimsuit, the others young men. The swimsuit and the trunks were all dripping wet—they'd just come out of the water. On this autumn day, the water was probably too cold for them. Along the whole coastline no one else was in the water. He had gone straight into the water without looking back, thinking that the woman might be watching him. He can't see them now. He looks back, toward the sun. It's setting, about to set behind the rehabilitation hospital's beachfront pavilion on the hill. The lingering brilliant yellow rays of the sun hurt his eyes, but he can see the beachfront pavilion on top of the hill, the outline of the hazy treetops above the coast road, and the boat-shaped rehabilitation hospital from the first floor up; anything below can't be seen, because of the surging sea and the direct rays of the sun. Are they still playing volleyball? He is treading water.

White-crested waves on the ink green sea. The surging waves surround him, but no fishing boats are at work. Turning his body, he is borne up by the waves. Up ahead on the gray-black sea is a dark spot, far in the distance. He drops down between the waves and can no longer see the surface of the sea. The sloping sea is black and shiny, smoother than satin. The cramp in his stomach gets worse. Lying on his back and floating on the water, he massages the hard spot on his abdomen until it hurts less. Diagonally in front, above his head, is a feathery cloud; up there, the wind must be even stronger.

As the waves rise and fall, he is borne up and then dropped between them. But just floating like this is useless. He has to swim quickly toward shore. Turning, he tries hard to keep his legs pressed together and, by so doing, counteract the wind and the waves to enhance his speed. But his stomach that had gained some slight relief again starts hurting. This time the pain comes faster. He feels his right leg immediately become stiff, and the water go right over his head. He can see only ink green water, so limpid and, moreover, extremely peaceful, except for the rapid string of bubbles he breathes out. His head emerges from the water and he blinks, trying to shake the water from his eyelashes. He still can't see the coastline. The sun has set, and the sky above the undulating hills glows with the color of roses. Are they still playing volleyball? That woman, it's all because of that red swimsuit of hers. He's sinking again, surrendering to the pain. He rapidly strikes out with his arms but, taking in air, swallows a mouthful of water, salty seawater, and coughing feels like a needle being jabbed into his stomach. He has to turn again, to lie flat on his back with his arms and legs apart. This way he can relax and let the pain subside a little. The sky above has turned gray. Are they still playing volleyball? They are important. Did the woman in the red swimsuit notice him entering the water, and will they look out to sea? That dark spot back there in the gray-black sea . . . is it a small boat? Or is it a pontoon that has broken loose from its mooring, and would anyone be concerned with what has happened to it? At this point, he can rely only upon himself. Even if he calls out, there is only the sound of the surging waves, monotonous, never ending. Listening to the waves has never been so lonely. He sways, but instantly steadies himself. Next, an icy current charges relentlessly by and carries him, helpless, along with it. Turning on his side, with his left arm stroking out, his right hand pressing against his abdomen, and his feet kicking, he massages. It still hurts, but it's bearable. He knows he can now depend only on the strength of his own kicking to fight his way out of the cold current. Whether or not he can bear it, he'll just have to, because this is the only way he'll be able to save himself. Don't take it too seriously. Serious or not, he has a cramp in the abdomen and he's one kilometer from shore, out in deep sea. He's not sure anymore if it's one kilometer, but senses that he's been floating in line with the coast. The strength of his kicking barely offsets the thrust of the current. He must struggle to get out of it, or else before too long he'll be like that dark spot floating on the waves, and vanish into the gray-black sea. He must endure the pain, he must relax, he must kick as hard as he can, he can't slacken off, and above all he mustn't panic. With great precision he has to coordinate his kicking, breathing, and massaging. He can't be distracted by any other thoughts, and he can't allow any thoughts of fear. The sun has set very quickly, and there is a hazy gray above the sea, but he can't see any lights on the shore yet. He can't even see the coast clearly, or the curves of the hills. His feet have kicked something! He panics, and feels a spasm in his stomach—sharp and painful. He gently moves his legs; there are stinging circles on his ankles. He has run into the tentacles of a jellyfish and he sees the gray-white creature, like an open umbrella, with thin floating membranous lips.

He is perfectly capable of grabbing it and pulling out its mouth and its tentacles. Over the past few days he has learned from the children living here by the sea how to catch and preserve jellyfish. Below the windowsill of his hostel window, there are seven salted jellyfish with their tentacles and mouths pulled out. Once the water is squeezed out, all that remain are sheets of shriveled skin, and he too will be just a piece of skin, a corpse, no longer able to float to the shore. Let the thing live. But he wants to live even more, and he will never catch jellyfish again— that is, if he can return to shore—and he won't even go into the sea again. He kicks hard, his right hand pressed against his stomach. He stops thinking about anything else, only about kicking in rhythm, evenly, as he pushes through the water. He can see the stars . . . they are wonderfully bright . . . in other words, his head is now pointing in the direction of the coast. The cramp in his abdomen has gone but he keeps rubbing it carefully, even though this slows him down. . . .

When he emerges from the sea and comes onto the shore, the beach is completely deserted. The tide is coming in again and he thinks he was helped by the tide. The wind blowing on his bare body is colder than it had been in the seawater, and he shivers. He collapses onto the beach, but the sand is no longer warm. Getting to his feet, he immediately starts running. He's in a hurry to tell people he's just escaped death. In the front hall of the hostel the same group is playing poker. They are all looking intently at the faces or at the cards of their opponents, and no one bothers to look up at him. He goes back to his own room, but his roommate, who is probably still chatting in the room next door, isn't there. He takes a towel from the windowsill, aware that the jellyfish, with a coat of salt on them and squashed under a rock outside his window, are still full of water. Afterward, he puts on fresh clothes and shoes and, feeling warm, returns alone to the beach.

The sound of the sea is all-embracing. The wind is stronger and lines of gray-white waves are charging onto shore. The black seawater suddenly spreads out, and because he doesn't jump in time, his shoes get soaked. He walks a little farther off, following the shore, along the dark beach. There is no longer any starlight. He hears voices, male and female, and the figures of three people. He stops. They are pushing two bicycles, and one of them has a girl with long hair sitting on the pillion. The wheel sinks into the sand and the person pushing seems to be struggling. But they keep talking and laughing; the voice of the girl sitting on the pillion is particularly happy. They stop in front of him, holding their bicycles. A young guy takes a big bag from the back rack of the other bicycle and hands it to the woman. They start taking off their clothes. Two skinny boys, stark naked and waving their arms, prance about, yelling: "It's really cold, it's really cold!" There is also the happy, cackling laughter of the girl.

"Do you want to drink it now?" asks the girl leaning on the bicycle.

They go over, take a wine bottle from the girl, take turns drinking from the bottle, pass it back to the girl, then run toward the sea.

"Hey! Hey!"

"Hey—"

The tide noisily charges forward and keeps rising.

"Hurry back!" The girl screams out, but it is only the crashing of the waves that respond.

In the faint light reflected on the sea surging up to the shore, he sees that the girl leaning on the bicycle is supporting herself on crutches.

THE ACCIDENT

It happened like this. . . .

A gust of wind swept up a pile of dirt from the roadwork outside Xinhua Bookshop on the other side of the road, swirled it up in an arc, then dumped it everywhere. The dust has just settled. It is five o'clock in the afternoon, right after the fourth beep has sounded on the radio in the radio repair shop in Desheng Avenue. It isn't the dust storm season and the weather is only starting to turn warm. Some cyclists are still wearing short gray cotton coats, although on the pavements there are already young women in pale blue spring clothes. There are endless streams of cyclists and pedestrians, but it isn't at a time when everyone is finishing work and traffic congestion is at its worst. However, inevitably there are people who are finishing work early, as inevitably there are people on work leave, so there are busy and idle people coming and going on the street. At this time of day it's always like this. The buses aren't too crowded even if all the seats have been taken and some people are standing, holding on to the handrail as they look out of the windows.

A bicycle fitted with an extra wheel for a baby-buggy with a red-and-blue checkered cloth shade is crossing diagonally from the other side of the road, and a man is riding it. Coming from the opposite direction is a two-carriage electric trolley bus that is going quite fast, but not too fast. It is clearly going more slowly than the small pale green sedan car about to overtake the bicycle, but neither is necessarily exceeding the city speed limit. The man on the bicycle arches his back, pedaling hard, and the little green car overtakes him on the other side. On this side, the trolley bus is heading toward him. The man hesitates but doesn't brake, and the bicycle with the buggy unhurriedly continues to cross diagonally. The trolley bus sounds the horn but doesn't reduce its speed. As the man crosses the white line in the middle of the road, the dust from the gust of wind has already settled, so his vision isn't obscured. Unblinkingly, he looks up; about forty, he is not a young man, and his hat, tilted slightly to the back of his head, shows that he is balding. He must be able to see the trolley bus coming toward him, and hear the horn. He hesitates again, seems to brake, although not hard, and the bicycle with the buggy clumsily continues crossing the road diagonally. The trolley bus is now close and the horn is sounding nonstop. However, the bicycle keeps going, as before. Sitting in the buggy under the shade is a child with rosy cheeks, barely three or four years old. Suddenly there is the screech of brakes and the horn sounds louder and louder as the trolley bus fast approaches. The bicycle's front wheel continues heading diagonally toward the bus, slowly, as the horn grows louder and the screeching of the brakes turns shrill. The bus has reduced its speed, but the front of the bus keeps moving ominously forward, closing in like a wall. The bus and the bicycle are about to collide and a woman on the pavement on this side of the road starts screaming. Pedestrians and cyclists alike all look on, but no one seems capable of moving. As the front wheel of the bicycle passes the front of the bus, the man starts pedaling hard, maybe he will just make it, but he reaches forward to touch the red-and-blue checkered shade, as if he is trying to push it down. As his hand touches the shade, the buggy flies off, bouncing on the single wheel. The man's legs are caught as he throws up his arms and falls backward off the bicycle. In the clamor of the horn and brakes and women screaming, before onlookers have time to gasp, the man is instantly crushed under the wheels. The bicycle he was riding, completely twisted, is thrown ten or so feet along the road.

The pedestrians on both sides of the road are aghast and cyclists get off their bicycles. It is quiet all around, and only the gentle singing from the radio repair shop can be heard:

You may remember
Our meeting in the mist, under the broken bridge . . .

It is probably a record of some post–Deng Lijun singer from Hong Kong. Front wheels in a pool of blood, the bus comes to a halt. Blood on the front of the bus is dripping back down onto the body. The first to approach the body is the bus driver, who has opened the door and jumped down. Next, people from both sides of the road also come running, while others surround the overturned buggy, which has rolled into the gutter. A middle-aged woman takes the child from the buggy, shakes it, and examines it all over.

"Is it dead?"

"It's dead!"

"Is it dead?"

Talk in low voices all around. The child, drained of color, has its eyes shut tight, and blue veins can be seen through the child's soft skin. But there is no sign of external injury.

"Don't let him get away!"

"Hurry, call the police!"

"Don't move anything! Don't go over there. Leave everything as it is!"

A crowd several layers deep has surrounded the front of the bus. Only one person is curious enough to lift the twisted wreck of the bicycle. The bell rings as he puts it back down.

"I clearly sounded the horn and braked! Everyone saw it; he was intent on getting himself killed by charging into the bus—how can you blame me?" It is the strained voice of the driver trying to explain, but no one takes any notice.

"You can all be witnesses, all of you saw it!"

"Move aside! Move aside—move aside, all of you!" A policeman with a big hat emerges from the crowd.

"We've got to hurry to save the child's life! Quick, stop a car and get the child to a hospital!" It is a man's voice.

A young man in a coffee-colored leather jacket runs to the line in the middle of the road, waving an arm. A small Toyota sedan sounds its horn nonstop to make its way through the pedestrians who have spilled onto the road-way. Next, one of those 130 light trucks comes along, and it stops. Inside the windows of the bus involved in the accident, passengers are bickering with the conductress. Another trolley bus pulls up behind. The doors of the one in front open and the passengers surge out, blocking the trolley bus that has just arrived. There is a loud clamor of voices.

I will never, never be able to forget . . .

The singing on the stereo is drowned out.

Blood is still dripping, and there is a stench of blood in the air.

"*Waaa . . .*" The child's repressed wailing finally breaks out.

"It's a good sign!"

"It's still alive!"

There are sighs of happy relief. As the wailing grows

louder, people also come back to life: it is as if they have been liberated. They then all rush to join the crowd surrounding the body.

Screaming sirens. A police car with flashing blue lights on the roof has arrived, and the crowd parts as four policemen quickly get out. Two of them are wielding batons, and people stand back immediately.

Traffic has come to a standstill and long queues of vehicles are waiting at both ends of the street. Honking horns have replaced the din of voices. One of the policemen goes to the middle of the road and waves his white-gloved hands to direct the traffic.

The police summon the conductress from the second trolley bus. She tries at first to make excuses, then reluctantly takes the child from the middle-aged woman and gets into the 130 light truck. A white glove signals. The truck drives off, taking with it the child's shrill screams and wailing.

As the police wielding batons shout at them, the onlookers move back to form a rectangle that includes the twisted wreck of the bicycle.

What is happening to the driver can now be seen from this side of the road. He is wiping off the sweat with his cotton cap. A policeman is questioning him. He takes out his driver's license in its red plastic folder, and the policeman confiscates it. He immediately protests.

"Why are you making excuses? If you've run over the

man, then you've run over him!" A youth pushing a bicycle yells out.

The conductress wearing sleeve-protectors comes out of the bus and rebukes the youth. "He was trying to get himself killed. The horn was sounding and the bus had braked, yet the man wouldn't give way. He just went under the bus."

"The man was in the middle of the road and had a child with him. It was broad daylight, so he must have seen him!" someone in the crowd says angrily.

"What does it matter to drivers like him if they run over someone? He won't have to pay for it with his life." This is said with derision.

"What a tragedy. If he didn't have the child with him, he would have got across long ago!"

"Is there any hope for the man?"

"His brain came out?"

"I just heard this *plop*—"

"You heard it?"

"Yes, it went *plop*—"

"Stop all this talk!"

"Ai, life's like that, a person can die just like that . . ."

"He's crying."

"Who?"

"The driver."

The driver, sitting on his haunches with his head down, has covered his eyes with his cap.

"He didn't do it deliberately . . ."

"If this had happened to anyone, they would . . ."

"The man had a child with him? What happened to the child? What happened to the child?" someone who has just arrived asks.

"The child wasn't hurt, it was very lucky."

"Luckily the child was saved."

"The man was killed!"

"Were they father and child?"

"Why did he have to hook a buggy to his bicycle? It's hard enough not to have an accident even with just one person on a bicycle."

"And he'd just picked up the child from kindergarten to take home."

"Kindergartens are hopeless, they won't let you leave children for a whole day!"

"You're lucky if you can get into one."

"What's there to look at! From now on, if you run without looking across the road—" A big hand drags away a child who is trying to squeeze between people in the crowd.

The Hong Kong star has stopped singing. People are crowded on the steps of the radio repair shop.

Red lights flashing, the ambulance has arrived. As medical personnel in white carry the body to the ambulance, the people in doorways of all the shops stand on their toes. The fat cook wearing an apron from a small eatery nearby has also come out to watch.

"What happened? Was there an accident? Was someone killed?"

"It was father and son, one of them is dead."

"Which of them died?"

"The old man!"

"What about the son?"

"Unhurt."

"That's shocking! Why didn't he pull his father out of the way?"

"It was the father who had pushed his son out of the way!"

"Each generation is getting worse, the man was wasting his time bringing up the son!"

"If you don't know what happened, then don't crap on."

"Who's crapping on?"

"I wasn't trying to start an argument with you."

"The child was carried away."

"Was there a small child as well?"

Others have just arrived.

"Do you mind not shoving?"

"Did I shove you?"

"What's there to look at? Move on! Everyone move on!"

On the outer fringes of the crowd people are being arrested. Traffic security personnel with red armbands have arrived and they are more savage than the police.

The driver, who is pushed into the police car, turns and tries to struggle, but the door shuts. People start to walk away and others get on their bicycles and leave. The onlookers thin out, but people keep arriving, stopping their bicycles or coming down off the pavement. The second trolley bus leads a long line of sedans, vans, jeeps, and big limousines slowly past the buggy with the torn red-and-blue checkered shade in the gutter on this side of the road. Most of the people standing on shop steps have either gone inside or left, and the long stream of cars has passed. At the center of what has become a small crowd in the middle of the road, two policemen are taking measurements with a tape measure, while another makes notes in a little notebook. The blood under the wheels of the bus has begun to congeal and is turning black. In the trolley bus with its doors open, the conductress sits by a window staring blankly across to this side of the street. On the other side of the street, the faces in the windows of an approaching trolley bus look out and some people even poke their heads out. People have finished work: it is peak traffic time, and there are even more pedestrians and people riding bicycles. However, shouts from the police and traffic security personnel stop people from going to the middle of the road.

"Was there an accident?"

"Was someone killed?"

"Must have been, look at all that blood."

"The day before, there was an accident on Jiankang Road. A sixteen-year-old was taken to the hospital, but they couldn't save him—they said he was an only son."

"Nowadays, whose family doesn't have only one son?"

"Ai, how will the parents survive?"

"If traffic management isn't improved, there'll be more accidents!"

"Well, there won't be any fewer."

"Every day after school, I worry until my Jiming gets home . . ."

"It's easier for you with your son—daughters are more worry to parents."

"Look, look, they're taking photographs."

"So what if they are, it's not going to help."

"Did he deliberately run over the man?"

"Who knows?"

"It couldn't have been attached, otherwise it would have been hit for sure."

"I was just passing by."

"Some drivers drive like maniacs, and aggressively. If you don't get out of the way, they certainly won't make way for you!"

"There are people who work off their frustrations by killing people, so anyone could be a victim."

"It's hard to guard against such occurrences, it's all decided by fate. In my old village there was a carpenter. He was good at his trade but he liked to drink. Once he was building someone a house and, on his way home at night, rotten drunk, he tripped and cracked his head open on a sharp rock . . ."

"For some reason, the past couple of days my eyelid has been twitching."

"Which one?"

"When you're walking you shouldn't be so engrossed in thought all the time. Quite a few times I've seen you . . ."

"Nothing's ever happened."

"If something had, it'd be too late and I wouldn't be able to bear it."

"Stop it! People are looking at us . . ."

The lovers look at one another and, holding each other's hands even more tightly, walk off.

They finish taking photographs of the scene of the accident, and the policeman with the tape measure takes a shovelful of dirt and spreads it over the blood. The wind has died down completely and it is getting dark. The conductress sitting by the window of the trolley bus has put on the lights and is counting the takings from the tickets. A policeman carries the wreckage of the bicycle on his shoulder to the car. Two men with red armbands get the buggy from the gutter, put it into the car, and leave with the policemen.

It is time for dinner. The conductress is left standing at the door of the trolley bus and looks around impatiently while waiting for the depot to send a driver. Passersby only occasionally glance at the empty bus stopped for some reason in the middle of the road. It is dark and no one notices the blood covered with dirt in front of the bus that can no longer be seen.

Afterward, the streetlights come on and at some time the empty bus has driven off. Cars speed endlessly on the road again and it is as if nothing has happened. By around midnight hardly anyone is about. A street-washing truck slowly approaches from the intersection some way off where traffic lights flash from time to time next to an iron railing with a blue poster. There is a row of words in white: FOR YOUR OWN SAFETY AND THAT OF OTHERS, PLEASE OBSERVE TRAFFIC RULES. At the spot where the accident had occurred, the truck slows down and, turning on its high-speed sprinkler jets, flushes clean any remaining traces of blood.

The road cleaners don't necessarily know that a few hours ago an accident had occurred and that the unfortunate victim had died right here. But who is the deceased? In this city of several million, only the man's family and some close friends would know him. And if the dead man wasn't carrying identification papers, right now they might not even know about the accident. The man probably was the child's father, and when the child calms down, it will probably be able to say the father's name. In that case, the man must have a wife. He was doing what the child's mother should have been doing, so he was a good father and a good husband. As he loved his child, presumably he also loved his wife, but did his wife love him? If she loved him, why wasn't she able to carry out her duties as his wife? Maybe he had a miserable life, otherwise why was he so distracted? Could it have been a personal failing and he was always indecisive? Maybe something was troubling him, something he couldn't resolve, and he was destined not to escape this even greater misfortune. However, he wouldn't have encountered this disaster if he had set out a little later or a little earlier. Or, if after picking up the child he had pedaled faster or slower, or if the woman at the kindergarten had spoken longer to him about his child, or if on the way a friend had stopped him to talk. It was unavoidable. He didn't have some terminal illness but was just waiting to die. Death is inescapable for everyone, but premature death can be avoided. So if he hadn't died in the accident, how would he have died? Traffic accidents in this city are inevitable, there are no cities free of traffic accidents. In every city there is inevitably this probability, even if the daily average is one in a million; and in a big city of this size there will always be someone encountering this sort of misfortune. He was one such unfortunate person. Didn't he have a premonition before it happened? When he finally encountered this misfortune what did he think? Probably he didn't have time to think, didn't have time to comprehend the great misfortune that was about to befall him. For him, there could be no greater misfortune than this. Even if he was that one in a million, like a grain of sand, before dying he had clearly thought of the child. Supposing it was his child, wasn't it noble of him to sacrifice himself? Maybe it was not purely noble but to a certain extent instinctual, the instinct of being a father. People only talk about a mother's instinct, but there are some mothers who abandon their babies. To have sacrificed himself for the child was indeed noble, but this sacrifice was entirely avoidable: if he had set out a little later or earlier, if at the time he had not been preoccupied, and if he were more resolute by nature, or even if he were more agile in his movements. The sum total of all these factors had hastened his death, so this misfortune was inevitable. I have been discussing philosophy again, but life is not philosophy, even if philosophy can derive from knowledge of life. And there is no need to turn life's traffic accidents into statistics, because that's a job for the traffic department or the public security department. Of course a traffic accident can serve as an item for a newspaper. And it can serve as the raw material for literature when it is supplemented by the imagination and written up as a moving narrative: this would then be creation. However, what is related here is simply the process of this traffic accident itself, a traffic accident that occurred at five o'clock, in the central section of Desheng Avenue in front of the radio repair shop.

BUYING A FISHING ROD FOR MY GRANDFATHER

I walk past a new shop that sells fishing equipment. The different fishing rods on display make me think of my grandfather, and I want to buy him one. There's a ten-piece fiberglass rod labeled "imported," though it's not clear if it's the whole rod that's imported or just the fiber-glass, nor is it clear how being imported makes any of it better. All ten pieces overlap and probably retract into the last black tube, at the end of which is a handle like a pis-tol's and a reel. It looks like an elongated revolver, like one of those Mausers that used to be in fashion. My grand-father certainly never saw a Mauser, and he never saw a fishing rod like this even in his dreams. His rods were bamboo, and he definitely wouldn't have bought one. He'd find a length of bamboo and straighten it over a fire, cooking the sweat on his hands as he turned the bamboo brown with the smoke. It ended up looking like an old rod that had caught fish over many generations.

My grandfather also made nets. A small net had about ten thousand knots, and day and night he would tie them nonstop. He'd move his lips while he knotted, as if count-ing or praying. This was hard, much harder work for him than the knitting my mother did. I don't recall his ever having caught a decent-sized fish in a net; at most, they were an inch long and only worth feeding to the cat.

I remember being a child, things that happened when I was a child. I remember that if my grandfather heard someone was going to the provincial capital, he would be sure to ask the person to bring back fishing hooks for him, as if fish could only be caught with hooks bought in the big city. I also remember his mumbling that the rods sold in the city had reels. After casting the line, you could relax and have a smoke as you waited for the bell on the rod to tinkle. He wanted one of those so he'd have his hands free to roll his cigarettes. My grandfather didn't smoke ready-rolled cigarettes. He ridiculed them as paper smokes and said they were more grass than tobacco, that they hardly tasted of tobacco. I would watch his gnarled fingers rub a dried tobacco leaf into shreds. Then all he had to do was tear off a piece of newspaper, roll the tobacco in it, and give it a lick. He called it rolling a cannon. That tobacco was really powerful, so powerful it made my grandfather cough, but that didn't keep him from rolling it. The cigarettes people gave him as presents he would give to my grandmother.

I remember that I broke my grandfather's favorite fishing rod when I fell. He was going fishing, and I had volunteered to carry the rod. I had it on my shoulder as I ran on ahead. I wasn't careful, and when I fell, the rod caught in the window of a house. My grandfather almost wept as he stroked the broken fishing rod. It was just like when my grandmother stroked her cracked bamboo mat. That mat of finely woven bamboo had been slept on for many years in our home and was a dark red color, like the fishing rod. Although she slept on it, she wouldn't let me sleep on it, and said if I did, I'd get diarrhea. She said the mat could be folded, so in secret I folded it, but as soon as I did, it cracked. I didn't dare tell her, of course, I only said I didn't believe it could be folded. But she insisted that it was made of black bamboo and that black bamboo mats could be folded. I didn't want to argue because she was getting old and I felt sorry for her. If she said it could be folded, then it could, but where I folded it, it cracked. Every summer the crack grew longer, and she kept waiting for a mat mender to come; she waited many years, but no mender came. I told her people didn't do this sort of work anymore and that she'd had the mat so long, she might as well buy a new one, but my grandmother didn't see it that way and always said the older, the better. It was like her: the older she got, the kinder she became and the more she had to say, by repeating herself. My grandfather wasn't like that: the older he got, the less he had to say and the thinner he became, until he was like a shadow, coming and going without a sound. But at night he coughed, and once he started, he couldn't stop, and I was afraid that one day he wouldn't be able to catch his breath. Still, he kept on smoking until his face and fingernails were the color of his tobacco, and he himself was like a dried tobacco leaf, thin and brittle, and it worried me that if he wasn't careful and bumped into something, he might break into little pieces.

My grandfather didn't just fish; he also loved to hunt. He once owned a well-greased shotgun made out of steel tubing. To make the shotgun was a lot to ask of anyone, and it took him half a year to find someone who would do it. I don't recall his bringing home anything except for a rabbit. He came in and threw a huge brown rabbit onto the kitchen floor. Then he took off his shoes, asked my grandmother to fetch hot water so he could soak his feet, and immediately started rubbing some tobacco he'd taken from his pouch. Wild with excitement, I hovered around the dead rabbit with our watchdog, Blackie. Unexpectedly my mother came in and started yelling. *Why didn't you get rid of that rabbit like I told you to? Why did you have to buy yourself that shotgun?* My grandfather muttered something, and my mother started yelling again. *If you must eat rabbit, ask the butcher to skin it before you bring it into the house!* My grandfather seemed very old then. After my mother left, he said German steel was good, as if with a shotgun made of German steel he could shoot something more than rabbits.

In the hills not far from the city, he told me, there used to be wolves, especially when the grass started to grow in the spring. Crazed with hunger after starving all winter, the wolves came into the villages and stole piglets, attacked cows, and even ate young cowherd girls. Once they ate a girl and left only her pigtails. If only he'd had a German shotgun then. But he wasn't able to keep even the shotgun he'd had made locally from steel tubing. In the book-burning era of the Cultural Revolution they called it a lethal weapon and confiscated it. He sat on a little wooden stool just staring ahead without saying a word. Whenever I thought about this, I felt sorry for the old man and dearly wanted to buy him a genuine German-made shotgun. I didn't, but I once saw a double-barreled shotgun in a sporting goods store. They told me I would need a letter of introduction from the highest-level sports committee in the province as well as a certificate from the public security office before they could sell it. So it was clear that I would be able to buy my grandfather only a fishing rod. Of course I also know that even with this imported ten-piece fiberglass fishing rod he won't catch anything, because our old home turned into a sandy hollow many years ago.

There used to be a lake not far from our home on Nanhu Road. When I attended primary school, I often passed the lake, but by the time I started junior secondary school, it had turned into a foul pond that produced only mosquitoes. Later, there was a health campaign and the pond was filled in. Our village also had a river. As I recall, it was in an area far from town, and when I was a child, I went there only a couple of times. Once when my grandfather came to visit, he told me that the river had dried up when a dam was built upriver. Even so, I want to buy him a fishing rod. It's hard to explain, and I'm not going to try. It's simply something that I want to do. For me the fishing rod is my grandfather and my grandfather is the fishing rod.

I step into the street shouldering a fishing rod with all its black fiberglass pieces fully extended. I can feel everyone looking at me and I don't like it. I'd like to get on a bus, where I won't be noticed as much, but I can't get the rod to retract. I hate it when people stare at me. Shy since childhood, I am uncomfortable in new clothes, and being dressed up is like standing in a display window; but it's worse carrying this long, swaying, shiny fishing rod. If I walk fast the rod sways more, so I go slow, parading down the street with the rod on my shoulder, feeling as if I've split my trousers or I can't zip up my fly.

Of course I know that people in the city who go fishing are not after fish. The men who buy tickets to fish in the parks are out for leisure and freedom. It's an excuse to escape from home, to get away from the wife and children, and to get a little peace. Fishing is now regarded as a sport, and there are competitions with divisions according to the type of rod used; the evening newspapers rate the sport highly and carry the results. Fishing spots and party venues are designated, but there are no signs of any fish. No wonder skeptics say that the night before the competitions, people from the fishing committee come to put fish into nets, and that's what the sportsmen catch. As I am carrying a brand-new rod on my shoulder, people must think I'm one of those fishing enthusiasts. But I know what it will mean to my old grandfather. I can already see him. So hunched over that he can't straighten his back, he is carrying his little bucket of worms. It is riddled with rust and bits of dirt are falling out of it. I should visit my old home to get over my homesickness.

But first I must find a safe place to put the rod. If that young son of mine sees it, he'll wreck it. I hear my wife shouting at me, *Why did you have to buy that? It's cramped enough in here already. Where will you put the thing?* I put it above the toilet tank in the bathroom, the only place my son can't reach, unless he climbs onto a stool. No matter what, I must go back to the village to get rid of this homesickness, which, once triggered, is impossible to shake. I hear a loud crash and think it's my wife using the meat cleaver in the kitchen. You hear her yelling, *Go and have a look!* You then hear that son of mine crying in the bathroom and know that calamity has befallen the fishing rod. You've made up your mind. You're taking the fishing rod back to your old home.

But the village has changed so much you can't recognize it. The dirt roads are now asphalt, and there are prefab buildings, all new and exactly the same. On the streets women of all ages are wearing bras, and they wear flimsy shirts to show them off, just as each rooftop must have an aerial to show there's a television in the house. A house without an aerial stands out and is regarded as defective. And of course everyone watches the same programs. From 7:00 to 7:30 it's the national news, from 7:30 to 8:00 the international, then short TV films, commercials, weather forecasts, sports, more commercials, then variety shows, and from 10:00 to 11:00 old movies. The movies aren't aired every day: on Mondays, Wednesdays, and Fridays, it's TV series instead. On the weekends, programs on cultural life are shown through the night. Anyway, the aerials are magnificent. It's as if the rooftops had grown small forests but a cold wind came and blew off all the leaves so that only bare branches remain. You are lost in these barren forests and can't find your old home.

I remember that every day on my way to school I had to pass a stone bridge, and the lake was right next to it. Even when there was no wind, there were waves lapping all the time, and I used to think they were the backs of swimming fish. I never imagined that the fish would all die, that the sparkling lake would turn into a foul pond, that the foul pond would then be filled in, and that I would not be able to find the way to my old home.

I ask where Nanhu Road is. But people look at you with surprise, as if they can't understand what you are saying. I still speak the village dialect, and anyone who does will always have a village accent. In our village, the word for grandfather is *laoye*. However, the word for "I," "me," or "my" is *wo*, produced between the back palate and the throat, and sounds like *e*, which means "goose." So *wo laoye* to a non-local sounds like "goose grandfather." And "goose" asking for directions using the back palate and throat fails to kindle any of that village friendliness in people. When I stop two young women and ask them, they just laugh. "Goose" doesn't understand why they're laughing. They laugh so hard, they can't answer, and their faces look like two pieces of red cloth. Their faces aren't red because they, too, are wearing bras, but because when I say "Nanhu Road," I also say *nan* between the back palate and throat, and it sounds funny to them. Later, I find an older man and ask him where the lake used to be. If I know where the lake was, it will be easy to find the stone bridge, and when I find the stone bridge, it will be easy to find Nanhu Road, and when I find Nanhu Road, I'll be able to feel the way to my old home.

The lake? Which lake? The lake that was filled in. Oh, that lake, the lake that was filled in is right here. He points with his foot. This used to be the lake. So we're standing on the bottom. Was there once a stone bridge nearby? Can't you see that there are asphalt roads everywhere? The stone bridges were all demolished and the new ones use reinforced concrete. You understand. You understand that what used to be no longer exists. It is futile to ask about a street and street number that used to exist, you will have to rely on your memory.

My childhood home had an elegant, old-style courtyard. The gate screen had a relief mural inlaid with carved stone images depicting Good Fortune, Prosperity, Longevity, and Happiness. Old Man Longevity, who had half of his head missing, held a dragon-head staff. The dragon's head had worn away, but we children were absolutely sure that Old Man Longevity's staff was in the shape of a dragon's head. The gate screen also had a spotted deer carved in it. The spots, of course, were those faint indentations on the deer's back. Whenever we went in or out we always touched the antlers, so they became very shiny. The courtyard had two entrances, one in front and one in the back. The bankrupt owner of the house lived in the back courtyard. There was a little girl in that family called Zaowa. She used to stare at me wide-eyed; it was funny but somehow sweet.

That courtyard definitely existed, as did the date trees growing there that my grandfather had planted. And the cages hanging in the eaves held my grandfather's birds in them. He kept a thrush there and even a mynah. My mother complained about the mynah being noisy, so my grandfather sold it and brought home a red-faced tit. But the tit died soon afterward; these birds are temperamental and shouldn't be caged. When my grandfather said that it was the tit's red face that made him fall in love with it, my grandmother scolded him for being shameless. I remember all this. The courtyard was No. 10 Nanhu Road. Even if they'd changed the name of the road and the number, they wouldn't have filled in this perfectly good courtyard, as they had that pond of foul water. But I ask everywhere and search street after street and lane after lane. I feel as if I'm rummaging through my pockets; I've taken out everything, but still can't find what I want. In despair I drag along my weary legs, uncertain whether they still belong to me.

Suddenly I have a brainstorm and remember Guandi Temple. It was in the opposite direction from the way I went to school, in the direction of the movie theater. When my mother took me to see a film we had to pass a lane called Guandi Temple. If I can find Guandi Temple, it won't be hard to work out the location of my home. So I start asking people how to find Guandi Temple.

Oh, so you're looking for Guandi Temple? What number? This confirms that Guandi Temple still exists. The person I encounter is so earnest and keen to help that he asks for the house number. Unable to think of a number right away, I mumble that I was wondering if the address still existed. If there's an address, of course it exists. Who are you looking for? What family do you want? He wants more details. Probably he thinks I'm back from overseas searching for my roots, or that I'm some drifter who abandoned his village. I explain that my family used to rent the house, and that it didn't belong to my grandfather. What was the name of the landlord? All I know is that the landlord had a daughter called Zaowa, but I can't tell him that.

As I continue mumbling, a scowl appears on the man's face and his eyes turn cold. He looks me up and down as if he's considering whether to report me to the police.

If you're looking for No. 1, go straight, then take the first lane on the right, it's on the south side of the road. If you're looking for No. 37, go that way, after about a hundred paces take the second lane, go to the very end, and it's on the north side, on the left. I thank him repeatedly, but when I go, I can feel his eyes boring into my back.

I see the first lane on the right, but before turning I see the brand-new blue road sign beside the red sign of the men's public lavatory. Written on it clearly and unmistakably is Guandi Temple, but this is not the impression I had of it as a child. I turn into the lane to show that I really did come to see my old home and am not up to any mischief. There is no need for me to look from No. 1 to No. 37. At a glance I can see to the end of the lane: it is not as long and winding as I remembered. I don't know whether or not a temple was there then. No tall buildings are on either side of the lane; rising above the old-style buildings is only one three-story redbrick building, an economy structure that seems less permanent than these old courtyards. Suddenly I remember that Guandi Temple burned down after being struck by lightning, but that was before I was capable of remembering anything. My grandfather told me about it. He said that the spot attracted lightning because the *qi* energies underground were in disharmony, so they built the temple to drive away the demons and evil spirits. Still it ended up being struck by lightning, proving that the site was not suited to human habitation. Anyway, my home was not in Guandi Temple, it was somewhere not too far from it. I must retrace the way my mother took me when I was a child. Having a child myself won't make it any easier, but I know that it's futile to keep asking people. I have gone in circles on the lake, beyond the lake, in the middle of the lake, around the lake, but if the sea can turn into mulberry trees, so too can this little lake. I suspect that my old home is hidden deep in the little forest of aerials in that stretch of old buildings, new buildings, and economy buildings that are neither old nor new, right in front of me. But no matter how much you keep going around them you can't see it. So you can only imagine it from your memories. It might be beyond that wall, converted to family dormitories by some urban environmental-protection authority. Or a plastic button factory might have turned it into a warehouse with iron doors and a guard, so unless you can state your business, don't even think about going in to nose around. Just tell yourself that people couldn't be so cruel as to demolish the gate screen with the carvings. But past and present sages and philosophers in China and the West believe that humans have a propensity for evil, and that evil is more deeply rooted than good in human nature. You like to believe in the goodness of people. People just wouldn't be so mean as to deliberately trample the memories of your childhood, because they too have a childhood worth remembering. This is as clear as one plus one cannot equal three. One plus one may change in quantity and substance, change into something grotesque, but it will never become three. To abolish such thoughts you must get away from these asphalt roads that all look alike, and away from these new buildings and old buildings, these blocks upon blocks upon blocks of half-new, half-old economy apartment blocks, under their forests of television aerials, bare branches devoid of leaves, as far as the eye can see.

I must go to the country, to the river where my grandfather took me fishing. He took me to the river, and although I can't remember if we caught any fish, I know I did have a grandfather and a childhood. I remember feeling awful when my mother made me take off all my clothes in the courtyard for a bath. I have also searched for the other houses I lived in as a child. I remember getting up in the middle of the night to go hunting, but it was not with my grandfather. After a whole day we killed a feral cat we thought was a fox. And I remember my poem in which I've strapped rattling hunting knives all over myself. I am a tailless dragonfly flitting over a plain, but the critic has barbed thorns growing in his eyes and a wide chin. I want to write a novel so profound that it would suffocate a fly.

I see my grandfather sitting on a small wooden stool, his back hunched, sputtering on his pipe. *Grandfather!* I call out to him, but he doesn't hear. I go right up to him and call again, *Grandfather!* He turns around but is no longer holding his pipe. Tears stream from his ancient eyes, which seem bloodshot from smoke. In winter, to get warm, he always liked to squat by the stove and burn wood. *Why are you crying, Grandfather?* I ask. He wipes the snivel with his hand. Sighing, he wipes his hand on his shoe but it doesn't leave a stain. He is wearing old cloth shoes with thick padded soles that my grandmother made for him. Without saying a word, he looks at me with his bloodshot eyes. *I've bought you a fishing rod with a hand reel,* I tell him. He grunts deep in his throat but without any enthusiasm.

I come to the riverbank. The sand underfoot crunches and sounds like my grandmother sighing. She is fond of chattering endlessly, although no one understands her. If you ask, *Grandmother, what did you say?* she will look up absentmindedly and, after a while, *Oh, you're back from school? Are you hungry? There are sweet potatoes in the bamboo steamer.* When she chatters it's best not to interrupt, she is talking about when she was a young woman, but if you eavesdrop from behind her chair, she seems to be saying, *It's hidden, it's hidden, everything is hidden, everything.* . . . All these memories are making noises in the sand under your feet.

This is a dried-up river, flowing with nothing but rocks. You are walking on rocks that have been rounded and smoothed by the river, and, jumping from rock to rock, you can almost see the clear current. But when the mountain floods came, an expanse of muddy water spread into the city. To get across the road, people had to roll their trousers up, and they kept falling in the brown slush where worn-out shoes and rotting paper floated. When the water receded, the bottom part of all the walls was covered with a sludge that, after a few days in the sun, dried into a shell and flaked off like fish scales. This is the river where my grandfather once took me, but now there is no water even in the gaps between the rocks. In the riverbed there are only unmoving big round rocks like a flock of dumb sheep huddled close to one another, afraid that people will drive them away.

You come to a sand dune with sinewy willow roots in it. The willows were cut, stolen, made into furniture, and then not a blade of grass would grow here. As you stand, you begin sinking, and suddenly the sand is up to your ankles. You must get away quickly or you will sink to the calves, knees, and thighs and be buried in this dune, which resembles a big grave. The sand murmurs that it wants to swallow everything. It has swallowed the riverbank and now wants to swallow the city, along with your childhood memories and mine. It clearly does not have good intentions, and I can't understand why my grandfather is just squatting there, not fleeing. I decide to make a hasty getaway, but a dune suddenly looms before me. Under the hot sun appears a naked child: it is myself as a child. My grandfather, in his baggy trousers, has risen to his feet. The lines on his face are no longer as deep, and he is holding the child's hand. The naked child, who is me, hops and skips at his side.

Are there any wild rabbits?

Mm.

Is Blackie coming with us?

Mm.

Does Blackie know how to catch rabbits?

Mm.

Blackie was our dog, but he disappeared. Some time later someone told my grandfather he saw Blackie's fur drying in a courtyard. My grandfather went there, and the people claimed that Blackie had killed their chicken. It was lies. Our Blackie was very obedient, and only once was he rough with our rooster and pulled out a few feathers. He was punished with a broomstick by my grandmother until he lay whining, front paws flat on the ground, begging for forgiveness. My grandfather was miserable, as if he had been beaten with the broomstick. The rooster was my grandmother's pet, and the dog went everywhere with my grandfather. From that time on, Blackie never bothered chickens, just as a good man never fights with a woman.

Are we going to run into wolves?

Mm.

Are we going to run into black bears?

Mm.

Grandfather, have you ever killed a black bear?

Grandfather grunts loudly but you can't tell whether it's a yes or no. I worshipped my grandfather because he had a shotgun, and it was really exciting when he filled his empty cartridges with gunpowder for it; I would pester him nonstop until he got cross. He seldom lost his temper, but once he did. He stamped his feet and yelled at me in a loud voice, *Go away! Go away!* I went inside, then suddenly heard an explosion. I was frightened and almost crawled under the bed, but finally I peeked out the door and saw that one of my grandfather's hands was covered with blood; his other hand was frantically wiping his face, which was all black. He was hurt, but he didn't cry.

Grandfather, are you also going to shoot a tiger?

Stop talking so much!

It was only after I grew up that I learned that real hunters don't talk much. My grandfather's hunting friends probably talked all the time, and that's why they didn't ever shoot anything; they also kept my grandfather, who didn't talk much, from shooting anything. When my grandfather was young, he came upon a tiger; it was in the mountains, not in a zoo. This happened in his old home, which was also my father's home, so it was my home, too. Back then, there were thick forests, but one time I passed my old home in a bus while on a work assignment. There were only bare brown slopes, and even the mountains had been turned into terraced fields. Those fields were once forests. The tiger looked at my grandfather and walked away. On television they say that in south China tigers have been extinct for more than ten years, except for those in zoos. Not only has no one ever shot a tiger in the wild, no one has even seen one. In the northeast there are still tigers: the experts estimate that there are at most a hundred of them. It's not known where they've hidden, and hunters would count themselves lucky if they saw one.

Grandfather, when you saw the tiger were you scared?

Bad people scare me, not tigers.

Grandfather, have you ever run into bad people?

There aren't many tigers but lots of bad people, only you can't shoot people.

But they're bad!

You can't tell right away whether they're good or bad.

What about when you can tell, can you shoot them then?

You would be breaking the law.

But aren't bad people breaking the law?

The law can't control bad people, because bad people are bad in their hearts.

But they do bad things!

You can't always be sure.

Grandfather, do we have far to go?

Mm.

Grandfather, I can't walk anymore.

Just grit your teeth and keep walking.

Grandfather, my teeth are falling out.

You bad boy, stand up!

Grandfather gets down on his haunches and the naked child climbs onto his back. With the boy on his back, he totters a step at a time in the sand, his feet turned outward. The boy whoops with joy and kicks his little feet, as if spurring on an old horse. You watch your grandfather's back gradually recede into the distance and sink behind a dune. Then there is only you and the wind.

Voller has three of his team protecting him. Their solid bodies form a barrier, and it won't be easy to take the ball from him. At the edge of the sand, a line of yellow smoke rises, and like an invisible hand it brushes the big dune into a roll of unfurling silk. You are in a desert. It is a dry sea to the horizon, burning red, still as death. You seem to be flying in a plane over the great Taklamakan Desert. The towering mountain range looks like the skeleton of a fish. The vast mountains will certainly be swallowed up in this burning, dry sea, yet in March the Taklamakan can be extremely cold. Those few blue circles are probably frozen lakes and the white edges are shallow beaches. The dark green spots that look like the eyes of dead fish are where the water is deep. In the second half of the match everyone can see that West Germany has stepped up its attack and is in the lead. Argentina will have to strengthen its defense; everything depends on how they counterattack and take advantage of gaps in the other side. Good kick! Valdano has the ball and he scores! There is no wind, just the gentle rocking of the motor. Outside the cabin window, there seems to be no horizon. The Taklamakan looms up diagonally in so straight a line that it could only be replicated on a blueprint; it divides the window into two. Following the line of vision and direction of flight, it moves clockwise from 0:50 to 1:20 or 1:30. At the end of the needle is a dead city. Is it the ancient city of Loulan? The ruins are right below and you can see the collapsed walls. The palaces have all lost their domes: here the ancient cultures of Persia and China once fused, then sank into the desert. Look everyone! Argentina is making a rapid counterattack and the other side can't keep up. Argentina scores a goal. In fifty-one matches in the series 127 goals were scored, and if you count the penalties in extra time, 148. In today's match, there were 2 more goals. Not counting the penalties in extra time, the 128th and 129th goals have been kicked. Now Maradona has the ball. Shifting sands and the ball. With is a loud howl, yellow shifting sand slowly forms a mound, then trickles down in waves—waves that rise, fall, and ripple outward, like breathing, like singing. Who is singing with a kind of sobbing under the shifting sands? You want desperately to dig it out, the sound right below your feet. You want to make a hole to let out this sound tinged with sadness, but as soon as you touch it, it twists and bores downward, refusing to come up. It's like an eel, and you catch only what seems to be a slimy tail that you can't hold on to. You dig furiously with both hands into the sand. On the riverbank you had to dig only a foot deep and water would percolate up—cool, pure, sparkling river water—but now there is just cold grit. You put your hand into it and feel a tingling sensation, then touch something sharp and cut your finger, although it doesn't bleed. You are determined to find out what it is. You dig and scrape and finally pull up a dead fish. The head was pointing down and it's the tail that cut you. Stiff and hard, the fish is as dry as the river: mouth clamped shut, eyeballs shriveled. You prod it, squeeze it, step on it, throw it, but it doesn't make a sound. It is the sand that makes a noise, not the fish, and it whispers to mock you. The dead fish, stiff in the blazing sun, sticks up its tail. You look away, but its round eye continues to stare at you. You walk off, hoping that the wind and sand will bury it. You won't dig it up again. Let it never see the daylight; let it stay buried in the sand. Burruchaga is offside, loses a great opportunity, and the defense kicks the ball out. In the second half Argentina gets a third corner but West Germany takes it, goes for a goal, and scores! At the twenty-seventh minute Rummenigge kicks it right at Maradona. The score is 1–2, and everyone sees Maradona taking his team toward the goal—

Grandfather, can you kick a soccer ball?

It's the soccer ball that's kicking your grandfather.

Who are you talking with?

You're talking with yourself, with the child you once were.

That boy without clothes?

A naked soul.

Do you have a soul?

I hope so. Otherwise this world would be too lonely.

Are you lonely?

In this world, yes.

What other world is there?

That inner world of yours that others can't see.

Do you have an inner world?

I hope so. It's only there that you can really be yourself.

Maradona is taking the ball past everyone. There's a goal! Whose is it? The score is 2–2, a draw for the first time. Doves of peace soar in the stadium. Seventeen minutes to the end of the match: time enough to have a dream. They say it only takes an instant to have a dream; a dream can be compressed into hardtack. I've eaten hardtack, dried fish in a plastic bag—without scales, eyes, or pointy tails that can cut your fingers. In this lifetime you can't go exploring in Loulan, you can only sit in a plane and hover in the air above the ancient city, drinking the beer served by the stewardess. The sound in your ears is music, eight channels on the armrest. Screeching rock and roll or a husky mezzo-soprano purring like a cat. Looking down at the ruins of Loulan, you find yourself lying on a beach; the fine sand flowing through your fingers forms a dune. At the bottom of the dune lies the dead fish that cut your finger without drawing blood. Fish blood and human blood have an odor, but dried fish can't bleed. Ignoring the pain in your finger, you dig hard and uncover a collapsed wall. It's the wall of the courtyard of your childhood. Behind it was a date tree, and once you sneaked off with your grandfather's fishing rod to knock down dates that you shared with her.

She walks out of the ruins and you follow, wanting to be sure that it is the girl with whom you had shared the dates. You can only see her back. Excited, you pursue her. She walks like a light gust of wind, but you can never catch up. Maradona is looking for a path, a path where none exists, and the other team watches him closely. He takes a fall, charges on, and now they are trying for a goal. It's in! You give a loud yell, and she turns around. It's the face of a woman you don't want to recognize. There are wrinkles on her cheeks, eyes, and forehead: a flabby old face without any color. You find it painful to keep looking. Should you smile? A smile might mock her, so you grimace, and of course it's not a pleasant sight.

Alone in the middle of the ruins of Loulan, you look around. You make out the brick room in the courtyard with the gate screen depicting Good Fortune, Prosperity, Longevity, and Happiness. It is where Blackie used to sleep and where my grandfather kept his little iron bucket for the worms: it is my grandfather's room. Before the wall collapsed, my grandfather's shotgun hung on it. That should be the passageway leading to the back courtyard, to Zaowa's home. Staring at me without blinking is a wolf crouched in the window frame of the collapsed wall of the back courtyard. This does not come as a surprise. I know that in the wilderness there is often little sign of human settlement, only wolves. But these crumbling walls around me are crawling with wolves. They have taken over the ruins. Don't look back, my grandfather once told me. A person attacked from behind in the wilderness must never look around. If he does, Zhang the Third will tear out his jugular.

I am scared stiff: these crouching Zhang the Thirds, treacherous bastards that attack from behind, are going to pounce, but I mustn't show that I'm frightened. The cunning animal at the window frame stands up like a person, resting its head on its right forepaw and watching me out of the corner of its left eye. All around, the wolves loudly smack their long tongues; they are losing patience. I recall how it was when my grandfather, as a young man, came face-to-face with a tiger in the paddy fields of his old home. Had he started to run, the tiger would have pounced and made a meal of him. However, I can neither retreat nor go forward, and can only bend quietly to feel in the earth with my hand. I find my grandfather's shotgun. Without hesitation, I raise the shotgun and slowly level it at the wolf before me. I must be like an experienced marksman, must not give them reason to think otherwise, must shoot them dead one at a time, not allowing my feet to get confused. I will start by shooting the wolf at the window, then turn left in a circle. Between each shot, I must work everything out in my mind. I can't hesitate or be careless. There were 132 goals in the 13th World Cup competition. The match is over; Argentina has beaten West Germany 3–2 and is the winner of the World Cup. I pull the trigger, and just as with the cornstalk shotgun my grandfather made for me when I was a child, the trigger breaks. The wolves roar with laughter, hooting and guffawing. Joyful shouts crash like waves at the Azteca Stadium in Mexico City, each wave higher. I am embarrassed, but I know that the danger has passed. These Zhang the Thirds are only people dressed as wolves, play-acting. Look, the players have been surrounded like heroes and are being lifted over everyone's heads. They're protecting Maradona, and he is saying, "Let me kiss all the children of the world." I hear my wife talking, and her aunt and uncle, who have come from far away. The soccer match, broadcast from early morning, is finished. I should get up to see if that ten-piece fiberglass fishing rod that I bought for my grandfather, who died long ago, is still on top of the toilet tank.

18 July1986, Beijing

IN AN INSTANT

He is alone, with his back to the sea, sitting in a canvas deck chair on the beach. There's a strong wind. The sky is very bright, without a trace of any cloud, and in the dazzling sunlight reflected against the sea, his face can't be seen clearly.

Big iron doors wet and streaked with rust, water from the top somewhere keeps dripping. The thick, heavy doors slowly open to either side and the gap in the middle widens. Police car sirens can be heard. Through the gap in the doors are towering buildings that block off the sun. One police car after another, and the nonstop sound of sirens.

In the dark passageway of the hall is a woman's back. Without switching on the light, she puts on an overcoat, hesitates, and puts her hand on the knob. She quietly opens the door and goes out. The knob turns softly and clicks as the door shuts.

The warm sun makes him drowsy. He closes his book, leans back in the chair, and puts on sunglasses: the two round lenses screen his eyes from the sunlight. Afterward, he covers his face with a broad-brimmed black hat, and he can hear nothing but the noisy waves of the sea.

The tide surges onto the beach, but before it can recede,

the sand soaks it up with a long hiss, so that all that is left is a line of yellowish froth.

His arms, hanging down, start to itch. Ants—first one, then one after another—are crawling up his arms.

She says when she made love with two men in front of the fire, it was very exciting. She is lying across the bed with her head to one side, eyes closed, outside the circle of light. The light is shining only on her long hair, and on her underwear and panty hose on the floor.

He senses the tide swelling. The seawater surges around the legs of the chair, swirls around, then recedes. An old tune fills the air. Beautiful and sad, it is like the wailing of a peasant woman at a funeral, and yet like the sobbing of a reed pipe.

She moves her ankles to kick off her shoes and bends to put on a new pair. A shoe with the heel worn to the quick lies discarded at the side of the passageway near the door.

A poster with a black-and-white photograph shows just the lower half of a woman holding up her long skirt and revealing her beautiful legs. She is standing on her toes. This is another advertisement for shoes, posted on the wall of the platform in the subway station. An old woman with a big empty bag is standing on the platform, a middle-aged man sitting on a bench is reading a newspaper. The train comes; some doors open and some don't. The people getting off head for the exit, and no one so much as looks at the advertisement. With his back turned, he is the only person left on the platform, and as others start to arrive, that back departs.

The legs of the deck chair are already immersed in the lapping water and the sea keeps rising. That sad tune is still playing, but it has become somewhat vague and sounds more like a reed pipe.

She says she wants a man twice her weight to bear down on her. In the dark she is lying on the bed, her eyes wide open. He is sitting at the desk, bare-chested, and without turning he asks if she will cope. She says she loves being squashed until she can't breathe and, having said this, she laughs. *Doo*—it's the computer.

The tune becomes louder and louder, yet more vague as well. It sounds like the wind tearing the paper used for windows, but with the grating of grains of sand mixed in. The tune becomes more vague, yet still hurts the ears a little. The sea has risen to the seat of the deck chair and it is swaying.

He is sitting at the computer with a cigarette in his mouth. A long sentence appears on the screen. "What" is not to understand and "what" is to understand or not is not to understand that even when "what" is understood, it is not understood, for "what" is to understand and "what" is not to understand, "what" is "what" and "is not" is "is not," and so is not to understand not wanting to understand or simply not understanding why "what" needs to be understood or whether "what" can be understood, and also it is not understood whether "what" is really not understood or that it simply hasn't been rendered so that it can be understood or is really understood but that there is a pretense not to understand or a refusal to try to understand or is pretending to want to understand yet deliberately not understanding or actually trying unsuccessfully to understand, then so what if it's not understood and if it's not understood, then why go to all this trouble of wanting to understand it—

A white-nosed clown in a circus troupe is playing an accordion, pulling and squeezing, pulling and pulling, squeezing and squeezing. He pulls the accordion out fully, gives a hard jerk, breaks the sound box, and the music instantly stops.

In the air, there is only the sound of the wind, the noisy waves of the sea, and the brilliant sunlight.

The ash on the cigarette is about to drop and, flicking it into the ashtray, he deletes each of the words of the uncompleted sentence one at a time.

A pair of hands shuffles a pile of mah-jongg tiles, takes one, feels it; it's a "middle," then there's a "develop," and a "white," and these are put in the sequence "middle" "develop" "white." Next to be picked up are "develop" "middle" "white" "develop" "middle" "white" "east" "develop" "middle" "wind" "north" "east" "south" "wind" "west" "north" "bamboo no. 2"—he pushes over the tiles and starts shuffling them again.

"Tell me a story!" He turns around and the table lamp

shines on the back of his head, and in the dark, on the bed, he sees her naked body curled up like a fish.

An empty chair is floating serenely on the water, as ripples of light are reflected on the waves. The sound of the tide can't be heard; only a long note vibrates in the air, sustained and monotonous.

A small boy is leaning on a wall, weeping and wailing, but there is no sound. The stone wall is covered with everlasting spring creeper and the sun is shining halfway up the wall.

On the clipped green lawn an elderly man wearing trousers with suspenders and a white shirt unbuttoned at the collar is pulling a length of rope. It is strenuous, but he is relaxed and unhurried.

He happens to stop in front of a glass advertising display on the street and then becomes absorbed with reading what is inside. The street is fairly deserted and only one or two pedestrians are out.

She is standing at the end of the street but there is an endless stream of cars. She is too impatient for the red light to change and starts weaving across the road. Another car speeds by and she quickly stops, retreating to the white line in the middle of the road. She looks in the direction of the approaching cars and runs across just after a small sedan has passed. On the footpath she goes up some steps, appears to stop to think for a while, then presses some numbers at the door. There's a buzz and she opens the door and goes inside. Before the door slowly closes, she turns around, but on that overcast day it is even more difficult to see her face clearly.

There is no chair in the water, only foam. The long-drawn-out sound is intermittent, yet remains suspended in the air, never completely cut off—there is only that bit of sound.

A fine drizzle is falling on the glass advertising display and he moves aside. The display is full of advertisements for houses on sale with prices attached, some with photographs, most are private residences in the country. Some of the houses are for rent, with ALREADY RENTED written prominently in red on the cheaper ones.

Another man comes along to pull the rope. He is dressed immaculately, wearing a tie, and he greets the old man wearing trousers with suspenders. Taking the rope and talking and laughing, he steadily sets about this chore. When a heavy thud comes from somewhere not far away, the second man scowls.

An empty mineral water bottle is floating on the sea, bobbing up and down upon the waves. All this time, the sunlight remains splendid and the sky is so clean, it looks unreal. Maybe because it is too clean, too bright, and too empty, and with the waves sparkling with sunlight, that the empty plastic bottle moving into the distance suddenly turns gray-black and looks like an aquatic bird or some other floating object. At some unknown time the intermittent, long-drawn-out sound has stopped and, like a thread of gossamer blown by the wind, has vanished without trace.

"A pair of swans came to this seaside, then only one of them was to be seen, the other must have been killed for a trophy. The one left behind flew away soon afterward." It is a woman's voice, and clearly for a man to hear. As she speaks, the floating object moving into the distance really looks like an aquatic bird.

A man wearing glasses comes along to watch the two men pulling the rope. He scrutinizes them with his glasses on, then, taking them off, he wipes them but doesn't seem to be able to see any more clearly. He can't tell if he is seeing clearly or if he is seeing, but not clearly. Nevertheless, unfazed about whether or not he's seeing clearly, he puts the glasses into his breast pocket and joins the ranks of the rope-pulling men.

He is standing in the middle of a deserted little street, a cobblestone road that crawls toward the main street. On both sides are old stone buildings and the shops downstairs either have their doors shut tight or have metal grilles in place. He looks up. On both sides, the curtains of all the windows upstairs are drawn. Everything is gloomy, except for a long narrow sliver of green-blue sky. At the place where the road and the sky meet, it is hard not to think that it is the sea.

Seagulls are circling in the sky, screeching noisily. Whether they have to screech like this to look for food or if it's out of sheer joy isn't clear, because they use a language not understood by humans. However, understanding or not is unimportant, what is important is that in the blue sky on this island they can soar as they will and can call out noisily.

Facing the long strip of clear blue sky carved out by the houses on both sides, his back view becomes a silhouette and his tie starts to flap. On the gloomy street this is the only thing moving.

She says she doesn't know what to do! Her voice is agitated. But he says coldly that he knows what he wants to do, but he can't. Sprawled on the bed in the dark, she sticks up her legs and kicks her feet against one another. He is sitting by the desk lamp typing on the keyboard, and on the screen appears: $? ! \# \rightarrow \sim \| \triangle \nabla I I U U \rightarrow \rightarrow \in ::$ $\sqrt{} \ \mathbb{C} \ne \int \equiv \measuredangle \odot \quad \therefore \approx \geq \quad \sigma \ ? \ \bigcirc \ \diamond \ \blacklozenge$

From behind, the only thing that can be seen moving is his tie. Going to the front to have a look, he sees that it is the faceless head of a jacket on a coat hanger, the hem of which is also moving in the wind. The stand for the coat hanger is on the footpath. No one is on the street, there are no vehicles, and all the shops are shut.

Screeching, a seagull swoops down and dives into the water. However, most of the seagulls are just sitting there, floating on the waves. Far out at sea, lines of white foam surge up. The sound of the waves is muffled, transmitted slowly, apparently traveling more slowly than the tide.

By the time the roar of the waves can be heard, the

seagull can be seen flying up from the water, neck extended and wings flapping, its eyes round and beady, its wings thrusting.

A round red apple with green streaks shines as if it has been waxed. Slowly and with precision it turns in the delicate hand of the woman examining it and is then put down.

Red wine, dark red like blood, in cut-crystal goblets on a table with a white tablecloth, the quiet sound of knives and forks. Behind the wine goblets is a phantomlike man in a suit and tie, and the bare shoulders and neck of an equally phantomlike woman wearing a necklace. The man is saying something but it can't be made out. He is apparently relaxed and happy.

The woman starts turning the apple again in her hand, and gradually the conversation at the table can be heard. Enthusiastic . . . Barbara . . . very interesting . . . won't you have some dessert . . . Lily, you're not eating much . . . thanks . . . really funny . . . what did he say . . . sorry . . . summer . . . an antique dealer . . . quite talented . . . went to Hong Kong . . . can't understand war . . . homosexuality . . . has a certain elasticity . . . indeed . . . is cute . . . news headlines . . . specializes in foot massages . . . sauna . . . doesn't possess his poise . . . why . . . best not to say . . . try telling . . . yesterday afternoon . . . she went crazy . . . is no longer usable . . . the kitten I have at home . . . too painful . . . maybe it's true . . . government . . . what surname . . . a variety of stout . . . discover . . . an absolute oaf . . .

The open bright red cassock on the statue of Buddha is painted with gold lines and decorated with reverse swastikas, the sign of myriad benevolence and good fortune. With his many-layered chin and his hands holding up his huge, round belly, he sits securely and sedately on the black marble altar above the incense burner on the wall. He is happy and contented, and his lips part in endless laughter. However, if one looks closer, he seems to be yawning, and if one looks again, his narrowed eyes make him seem to be dozing off. On further scrutiny he is glaring horribly.

He goes into a bar and sits on a tall stool. The waiter brings two big glasses of beer and puts them on the counter in front of him. Quite a few are in the bar but it's not too crowded, and in the bright blue light, people's faces can't be seen clearly. They are all drinking and keep to themselves. A piano stands in the light on a small platform, and a black woman is playing. It is jazz blues and very melancholy. Old and ugly like a toad, from time to time she touches the keys, solicitously, fondly, as if caressing her lover. The black man nearby with a wreath of gray crinkled hair on his head is old like her, but he hasn't aged too badly. He is playing on several drums as he sings a sentence or a half into the microphone.

A good fire is burning and the wood crackles quietly; close up, the sound of the wind drawn down into the chimney can be heard. The black marble fireplace is spotless and the shag carpet goes right up to it.

At this point a fourth person arrives. He is wearing a leather jacket. Without a word he too proceeds to pull the rope. The men are all conscientious, unflustered, and the rope is pulled taut. They move forward, one upturned hand after the other, and keep persevering, but it is very strenuous.

"A Chinese guy . . ." the old black man is singing in English, but doesn't look at him. The old black woman runs her fingers rapidly over a set of keys, bending over the piano and swaying drunkenly, totally absorbed in the music, and also not looking at him. He keeps to himself and goes on drinking his beer. In the dark blue light no one looks at anyone else, entranced as they are by the music, like a crowd of nodding puppets.

The horse rears its hairy hooves. "Wandering all over the world . . ." sings the old black man.

The hands of the old black woman come down hard on the keys and there's a boom as the ground shakes under the horse's hooves. "Wandering all over the world, wandering all over the world . . ." As the old man sings, he plays the drums, and people nod to the beat.

The rope edges forward as the men pull on it, one hand after the other, straining their feet inside their shoes against the green grassy ground.

The spray splashes high as waves crash against the seawall. The waves under the seawall surge up and the beach can no longer be seen. The sunlight has the same intense brilliance, but the sky and the sea appear bluer.

One end of the rope finally appears. The fishhook, painted a bright red, has a huge dead fish hooked to it, and it is dragged onto the green grass. The fish on the hook has its mouth wide open and seems to be gasping futilely for air. The fish's wide-open eyes have lost their shine and have a dazed look.

The seawater spills over the seawall and trickles down the other side. The sky turns dark blue and the sunlight seems to be even more strangely transparent.

A big cockroach with shiny wings and trembling feelers runs onto the milk white shag carpet and crawls over the twisted threads of wool. The hanging lamp casts a circle of light on the rear of a beautifully carved mahogany horse: its glossy round rump, its hind legs, and its hooves shod with little red brass nails.

"Wandering . . . all over the world! Wandering . . . all over . . . the world!" The piano keys sing in response to the wrinkled old black hands. The man moves his head to the music. On the counter in front of him are three empty beer glasses, and in his hand he has another half-empty glass. A white woman sits on the tall stool next to him. Her bottom, wrapped in a tight, short leather skirt, is round and shiny, like the horse's rump.

Seawater like black satin is spilling over the seawall; at the foot of the wall in the spreading seawater lies a dead fish. There is an absence of sound. The tide and wind have suddenly stopped. Time seems to have frozen. Only the sea, like a length of spreading black satin, is flowing and yet not spilling. Maybe it isn't moving and only seems to be flowing, merely offering the sensation that it is flowing and only sensed as a visual image.

His hand squashes a fleeing cockroach on top of the electric stove. He turns on the tap but doesn't flush it away. Instead he just looks at the splashing water.

"Want marijuana?" The voice is low, so low that it is mistaken for breathing because the music is very loud. As wrinkled black hands fly across the keys, they seem to be the words of the song softly repeated. But the old black man is not singing; head down, he sways as he continues to play the drums.

The shiny brass bomb hanging on a fleshy earlobe of the white woman swings gently.

Cockroaches are crawling on the patterned tiles over the sink, crawling on the lid of the enamel saucepan, crawling on the leather cover of the radio, crawling on the cupboard, crawling along the kitchen door. He puts on a rubber glove.

A big hand with blue veins is on the woman's thigh, under the black leather skirt. Who does it belong to, and where is he? Is the old black man still playing the drums, is the piano still playing? Where is that pinging noise coming from? Anyway, everything seems to be swaying.

An eye, the dazed, cold gray eye of a fish, round and staring, dull and lusterless.

A pair of pointy pliers pulls out a tooth, the pale blood still clinging to the roots. He sniffs at it, it stinks a bit, and with a swing of his arm he tosses it away.

People are mountain climbing. Everyone is trying to outdo the other and it seems to be a race up the mountain. There are men and women, some wearing shorts, some carrying backpacks. There are also old and young people, some have walking sticks and some have small children, and pairs of boys and girls are holding hands, so it doesn't seem to be a race. Everyone has been mobilized. Is it a holiday camp or are they the residents of the whole county town? It suits everyone, men and women, old and young; is it a trendy form of exercise?

Cockroaches are crawling everywhere. Wearing a glove covered with dead cockroaches, he is on his haunches, frantically swiping at them.

Two feet in pointed leather shoes are stepping about in midair. On the stage, a white-nosed clown is walking on his hands to the tune of a leaky accordion soundlessly oozing air.

Everyone is puffing and panting, sweating from their foreheads. All of them take out identical bottles labeled with the same brand of mineral water and, one by one, their broad, contorted faces produce similar smiles of well-being.

A hat spins silently on the end of a walking stick.

The wind is taking a break, and on the boundless sea the layers of white crests keep pushing closer and closer.

The sunlight is wonderful, the sky remains azure blue, and the seagulls are screeching.

People are marching in file along the mountain ridge. The person in the lead is holding a tattered old flag that billows in the strong wind. They are off in the distance, but the flapping of the tattered flag can still be heard.

The sea swells up to the stone steps beyond the doors, majestically, turbulently.

The ground is thick with cockroaches. He stands still, and bends his head to look around. He is utterly frustrated and can do nothing but take off the glove that is covered with dead cockroaches.

Without a sound, the sea spills over the doorsill into the room, and the cockroaches scramble to escape by crawling up the walls. Those not quick enough are caught in the swirling current and float up with it or lie on their backs pretending to be dead. He can't help bending to look at them. He pokes at them with the glove, then throws it into the water, straightens up, and doesn't bother with them anymore. The legs of the table and chair are underwater and some of the cockroaches in the water start crawling up them.

The people with the flag are marching in file along the gentle ridge. As they draw near, the man in the lead raises his walking stick high. The flag flapping noisily in the wind is in fact a string of bras—white silk, dark red brocade, flesh-colored netting—all tied together with black nylon stockings. A small black leather bra shakes up and down from time to time and looks like a small bird trying to break free.

A large part of the concrete ceiling is wet, and the pooling water forms droplets that begin to fall.

In the underground cellar, someone is lying faceup on a mattress so old that it should be thrown away. His face is covered with a black hat, and his body is covered with a white sheet; the mattress is right in the middle of four wet concrete walls. Drops of water plop noisily onto the sheet and part of it gradually becomes wet.

His fat belly is exposed, covered only with bamboo medical suction cups; the part below his lower abdomen is covered with the white sheet.

Sitting on a small wooden stool, a cobbler wearing a felt hat takes the nail from between his teeth and presses it into the high heel of the shoe clamped between his knees. With one blow of the hammer, it is in.

The murky black seawater flows down from the stone steps, soundlessly, flowing down, one step at a time.

He looks up to the ruins of the fortress at the top of the cliff and goes up the broken stone steps that are in the shadows. The fortress, however, is in the sunlight and the outline and texture of each stone are quite distinct.

He enters the pitch black doorway of the fortress wall, then suddenly hears the sound of an iron chisel being hammered into rock. He stands still and the sound stops.

As soon as he resumes walking the sound follows his footsteps. He stops and the sound stops again. He then deliberately stamps his feet and the iron chisel clangs noisily. Finally, when he starts running hard, the sound vanishes.

It is a long, dark tunnel. He moves slowly ahead, groping. At the other end is a ray of light and the exit gradually appears—a doorway. Outside, the sunlight is brilliant, and the sound of the chisel can be heard clearly. Moving stealthily to the doorway, hiding in the shadows, he sees someone hammering at some rocks. He walks over and stops behind the man. The man turns around. He has a dry, sunken, old face creased with deep wrinkles, yellow and tanned, and his sparse front teeth are completely covered with tobacco stains. He is an old Chinese peasant from a mountain village and as he squints in the sunlight, his eyes are vacant in the slits, staring somewhere else. The vague sound of the sea vanishes just as it starts.

The murky black seawater surges in from the stone steps above on the left, soundlessly. A little light comes in only from outside the half-open doors above the stone steps, and the reflected light indicates that the force of the water is quite strong.

He is pedaling on a bicycle and the wheels are turning at a medium pace. He is riding an ancient bicycle with wide handlebars, traveling along a narrow village highway. In the distance on the left is a big stretch of grassland on a slight incline where there is a line of four people, backs bent, who seem to be pulling hard on something. What they are pulling isn't clear, but it is something very heavy that looks like a wooden boat yet could be a coffin, and leaves a track in the grass wherever they pass. Their every step is slow and strained. Wafting through the air is a woman's wail, like song and lament, like the wailing of a Chinese peasant woman at a funeral.

The sun reflecting off the bell on the bicycle handlebars hurts his eyes, and the wailing seems more and more like the songs or hauling chants of coolie workers. The wheels of the bicycle turn along the straight asphalt road.

Four gaunt men with purplish bronze faces, sweating backs, and bare upper torsos are wearing wide cloth waistbands and straw sandals. As he looks at the rope, which appears to be taut, there is a sudden loud snap.

A motor car overtakes the bicycle, and speeds off. As he turns his head to look back, the sun directly over the left side of the field is blinding. No one is around and the lingering sound seems to be either the cry of insects or his ears ringing.

In the underground cellar, the mattress is soaked in the black water. The white sheet is also saturated, and the man with a hat over his face is stiff and looks like a corpse. Water keeps dripping from above, and there is now also the pop of bursting bubbles.

With the bicycle parked nearby, he lies on his side in the shade of a tree, looking at this neglected apple orchard. Here and there among the branches are a few red apples that had escaped being picked. Not too far away is the gurgling of a creek.

A barefoot girl appears under the apple trees ahead. She is carrying a bucket of water that seems too heavy for her. Her purplish red jacket has a single slanting lapel, and the legs of her blue floral-print trousers are rolled up to just below the knees. She has two long plaits, and her bright black eyes look too big for her small face. She gives a start, uncertain whether or not to keep walking. Suddenly it is lonely all around.

A small tree is drifting in the wind. Dirt splashes up, and billowing clouds of thick black smoke and dust suddenly spread through the sky. Then, as planes swoop overhead, the strafing of machine guns, exploding bombs, and, immediately afterward, the crying of babies and the wailing of women can be heard.

Several small boys squat around an iron spade, watching it sink into the ground as a foot treads down on it. A clod of earth is dug up and flattened into small pieces with the spade, then another clod of earth is dug up and flattened, and yet another. A big boy stoops to pick up a machine-gun bullet, brushes it on his shirt, puts it into his trouser pocket, then takes the spade to another hole nearby to dig. One of the small boys surrounding him shakes his head as he looks at the row of holes in the ground.

The murky black water makes a gurgling sound as it flows down all the stone steps, unstoppably.

A match is struck in the dark and a yellowing, slightly

faded old photograph is set alight. It is the photograph of a young man in a suit and tie and a young woman in a *qipao* together with a three- or four-year-old boy. Their shoulders pressed together, both the adults have posed smiles on their faces. The eyes of the boy between the parents are rounded, and he has a surprised look. The flames on the edge of the photograph are burning toward his parents. The photograph is shrinking and beginning to curl up, then—*whoosh!*—the whole photograph is burning, his parents are alight and the child is charred.

A bubble keeps growing as it is blown. The soapy surface is moving faster and with the sun shining on it, the colors become brighter, more colorful, more sparkling, until it can't get any bigger. It silently bursts as amazement lights up the face of the little boy blowing bubbles.

The mattress in the black water slowly begins to float up. It tilts slightly, wobbles back, sways a few times, each time becoming steadier, and eventually it is floating on the water.

Water is dripping everywhere. He looks up at the rainwater coming down from the eaves; outside on the ground there are some abandoned iron plows and farm machine parts. Two dogs charge at him with their jaws wide open. He retreats into the granary, where the ceiling is high and bundles of fodder are stacked right up to it. There is a long wooden bench in the middle of the dark granary and young women are sitting around it. All of them have flour sticking to different parts of their faces: eyelids, nose, eyebrows, cheeks, lips, ears. Heads bowed, they shape lumps of dough in their hands as they chant, engrossed in grief. However, a young woman with long plaits has an oil lamp with a shade in front of her. She is looking into a mirror at her woman companion behind who has untied her plaits and is combing her hair for her. Without realizing it, he is right by the mirror and sees the scissors cut her long hair short. Immediately, the barking of dogs is heard.

Rainy weather, an empty lane in a village that is so lonely, it is hard even to hear the rain. Above the stone wall is a row of tightly shut old wooden windows. A small wooden door reinforced with iron strips set into the stone wall stands as tall as a person on the cobblestone road. Dried by wind, the rough grain sticks out on the timber. The sad song of a girl weeping at being married seems to seep faintly through the cracks of the door. As one approaches the door, everything becomes more and more hazy.

Hands slowly push open a heavy door, inside is a church. The rows of empty pews retreat in the midst of the reverberating footsteps echoing on the stone floor. On the walls are the remains of medieval murals. The lines are blurred, the colors blackened with grime, and none of the crumbling faces of the disciples can be made out.

A mountain creek with rounded pebbles and a fast-flowing current. He looks back. In the gray drizzling rain, opposite, on the mountain slope is a village connected by stone steps; it has a church with a prominent bell tower. The rain is falling even more heavily.

He is walking on the village highway, his clothes almost soaked through, and water is running down the back of his head. As a car drives past, he signals. It has gone ten paces past him, but stops. He quickly runs up and a door opens.

A woman is driving. From the rearview mirror the woman's profile can be seen: she has wrinkles at the corners of her eyes. She asks him something and he answers. The woman turns to look at him. She really knows how to use her makeup. The woman asks him something again and he answers again. The woman looks away, but in the rearview mirror there is the suggestion of a smile at the corners of her mouth. The car windows swept by the rain are dripping with water.

The murky seawater goes over the steps behind the doors and continues to surge inside. In the light behind the doors it looks more like black satin running off a roll and cascading down.

Looking down, he sees naked men and women on a long table. They are huddled in couples and move up and down and turn around endlessly, as drops of milk white flour and water splash onto the table and their bodies, making a sound like pattering rain. All around are bundles of straw; it seems to be a granary, yet from time to time there is snorting, and it seems to be a stable.

He is sitting at an old round table wearing a pair of

dark blue swimming trunks. Both of his hands are on the shiny grain-patterned hardwood surface, one of them turning a glass half filled with red wine. A hanging lamp with a metal shade casts a yellow light that shines only on his hands. In the circle of light there is also a highly polished stone ball that leaves a distinct shadow on the table. He withdraws the hand with the wineglass from the circle of light, and his other hand moves the stone ball so that from that position the shadow is extended. Music instantly starts up. It seems to be jazz blues, trembling and restrained, intermittent, powerful yet weak, seemingly far and yet near, and finally it stops abruptly, yet seems still to be suspended there. . . . He gets to his feet and walks around the table, observing the endless positions of the stone ball and its shadow in the circle of light.

Next to the white curtain, a wall lamp illuminates the portrait of a woman on the wall, with black lips, fair skin, black hair piled high on the head, eyes looking down, lips slightly parted, and looking almost asleep. On closer scrutiny, it turns out that one eye is open and the other is shut, and if one takes a step back, it would seem that one eye is higher than the other. To look up at an angle, one would see that the lower lip is thick and fleshy. But looking at it sideways, one would see that the lips are pouting. Another look would make it seem like the wide-open mouth of a bird. An upside-down look would make the tongue seem to stick out. Away from the light, there are

knife marks all over the cheeks: it is a shaman with an evil
look. A look with eyes narrowed and with an air of indif-
ference would return the sexiness to the face. There is a
pop as the light goes out.

A gurgling sound, water is flowing down the stone
steps in places. Now and then a dim light flashes a few
times.

The curtains open noisily. A woman's bare back appears
in front of the curtains. She opens the window, and outside
is a mass of gray rooftops. Farther off, one after the other,
are endless balconies and apartments of old buildings. The
dark blue sky is unusually clear, but it could be morning or
dusk. The woman turns and leans on the laced wrought-
iron railing outside the window, wearily. Her face and body
are in the dark and only her eyes glint, like a cat's eyes in the
dark. A bracelet on the wrist of her hand that grips the railing also has a faint glint. A car speeding by brings with it the
rumbling of the waves.

Seagulls circle the sea, screeching, as if they have found
something and are following the rising and falling of the
waves. The waves are huge, and between the crests are
expanses of smooth, deep blue sea.

Underfoot is withered grass, swaying in the strong
wind, soundlessly. He is walking on a mountain slope and
he goes behind the ruins of a wall where a few young people are waiting for him. One of them is wearing glasses,
and the thick lenses for severe shortsightedness look like

fish eyes. Another, a young woman with short hair and dark complexion, is eating melon seeds. She spits out the shells that float and then drop into the clumps of grass. Seeing him arrive, without a word, they head down the slope together. Below is a cluster of houses, a bell tower, and a football field.

In the underground cellar that has filled with seawater, the mattress soaked in murky water slowly floats up. The faint rumble of cars driving past sounds like the wind.

The young people go into a long corridor where sections of sunlight broken by pillars appear unusually bright. It is a classroom with the doors and windows wide open but empty of people. It is filled with tables and chairs that pass them, one by one, as their footsteps sound after they have passed.

At the end of the corridor is a room. The door is shut but there is a sign. They come to a halt and look at the sign that has nothing written on it, hesitate, seem to be having a discussion, then knock on the door. It opens instantly, soundlessly. Inside the room, teachers are sitting at desks as if they were students, all busy marking homework. While they are wondering whether to ask someone, a young teacher appears behind them. She is as young as she was in those times, only her face is pale and she looks to be made of wax. Fatigue shows all over her face; her eyes are puffy and have grayish shadows. She says she will escort them to the principal and also says she is delighted that, so many years after graduating, they have come to visit their old school. She says she remembers the class, back then they were all children but full of mischief. As she talks and jokes, her voice is coming from a paper person. Of course she remembers the time when there was a cruel struggle right on those very desks. Someone had started banging on a desk and everyone unthinkingly followed, so that every desk was banging. As she mounted the dais, textbooks under her arm, her rounded eyes swept the class, but she couldn't isolate the ringleader. Confused, she threw down her textbooks and ran out in tears. Everyone was scared stupid, then suddenly it was quiet and nobody made a sound.

There is a red-colored cross on the door of the medical clinic in the passageway. She points to the window. The small, dark room is piled with junk as well as some musical instruments—*erhu*, *pipa*, gongs, and drums—all of them covered in dust. He knows that this used to be where students were kept after class as punishment for failing to hand in homework. Those passing the window can see that miserable desk scarred with knife cuts and covered in ink stains and pencil marks.

He stares at the desk for some time and, from where he is looking, there clearly emerge, one on top of the other, pencil drawings of little people and little crooked houses as well as Chinese characters carved with a penknife. Some of the character strokes have been inked in, and some inked characters where the ink couldn't be scrubbed clean had been penciled in and again carved with a penknife. It is a jumbled picture but it conjures up fantasies.

The sound of water dripping, dripping in the cellar filled with seawater, dripping on the floating mattress, dripping and soaking the sheet. And the ink black seawater keeps rising, soundlessly. The floating mattress hits a soggy wall, bounces, and changes direction.

The principal, who has a dark, ruddy complexion, a big Adam's apple, and a husky voice, tells them the history of the school. His low drone reverberates around the ridgepole and rafters of the big temple-like ceiling above the auditorium, filled with long wooden benches. Bells start ringing, and the sparrows fly off in fright.

Below the ceiling are several Taoists clad in long gray cotton gowns, their hair in topknots. Heads bowed and hands clasped in front, the one in the lead swinging a horsetail whisk, they are chanting scriptures around a coffin.

The lid of the coffin is open and he almost guesses that the corpse in the coffin, with its head wrapped in the shroud, is himself. Apparently confused, he turns and looks around, although he doesn't know what it is he is looking for. However, he sees behind him two big heavy doors that are half-open, and outside in the sun, on the stone steps, a little wooden bucket with peeling paint. A lizard is crawling on the stone step in front of the wooden bucket.

He walks out of the auditorium, or maybe it was originally a temple that had been converted into a school auditorium, or maybe it was in fact a temple hall. In the shadows of the covered walkway stands an old stone tablet with parts missing. It looks like the wild-grass calligraphy of Mi Di, but the inscription in very standard regular script reads: "Written by Meng Chun in the *ding-mao* year of the reign of Yuanyou of the Great Song Dynasty." Long ago, ink rubbings were made of it, but later the main piece of calligraphy was engraved over and now can barely be made out and is completely undecipherable.

He walks out into the sun. A boy in a vest and shorts, riding on a brand-new Dinglan junior bicycle, passes by. He asks the boy something. The boy stops and, with a foot on the grass, points ahead, then speeds off.

He walks on ahead and passes a piece of neatly trimmed lawn. Past the lawn, in a mass of weeds, are the shiny handlebars of a bicycle. He goes over to have a look, and covered with weeds in the ditch is the frame of a Dinglan bicycle.

He strides quickly up the hill, begins to run, and then runs faster and faster, panting hard, but in his mind he seems more and more to understand that he is surely pursuing the self of his childhood. On the top of the hill is a sour-date tree, though not a very tall one, with its small leaves trembling in the wind.

The child is running in his direction from behind the hill but stops in front of the sour-date tree and looks about with a worried look. Then, probably discovering some-thing, he dashes off somewhere else. Not far from the top of the hill is a small, sparse forest where between two trees a white bed sheet is drying; something seems to be moving behind the sheet, and the child charges headlong into the sheet but gets wrapped in it and can't get free.

The mountain wind is toying with the sheet. Out of breath and with great difficulty the child manages to lift the sheet and get out, only to find yet another sheet hang-ing between two trees and flying about.

The child stares for a while, then quietly walks over to it. There seems to be the shape of a person behind the sheet. This time the child carefully and gently lifts a corner of the sheet. Nothing is there, but nearby, another sheet is hanging between two trees. Instinctively, the child looks behind himself.

All around, far and near, sheets are swirling in the wind. Stopping in front of one, he sees the legs of a woman emerging on the white sheet, and he holds his breath to examine the heaving white breasts with protruding nipples. Then, roughly separating the sheets, he comes face-to-face with the child standing among the white curtains with a ter-rified look in his eyes. There is a loud scream, the sound of the *suona*, and he covers his face with his hands.

Crawling from the front of the coffin covered in white streamers, the child runs off wailing and howling, and echoing this silent weeping is the long, drawn-out scream of the *suona*. When the sounds of the child and the *suona* vanish, there remain around the open coffin only white curtains and paper streamers drifting in the wind.

The gloomy sea keeps rising and the wet mattress is partly floating on the water. The black hat over his face gets closer and closer to the ceiling of the room.

He leaps out of the coffin that is covered in long paper streamers and, dragging the shroud with him, he staggers and stumbles as he flees this mountainside with paper streamers hanging all around. He runs down to the expanse of green lake in the valley, enters the water, plunges into the lake, and somehow becomes tangled in weeds and is struggling. In the distance, ripples are spreading in circles, but it is hard to tell whether he is drowning or swimming out to the middle of the lake.

The sea reaches the ceiling, gurgling like a drowning person who is swallowing water and giving off bubbles like a blocked underwater pipe.

The watery passage grows bluer and bluer and eventually comes out at a seaport with sparkling waves. In the distance, the sea and the sky are virtually one color.

A gray-black floating object is bobbing up and down on top of the waves. As the tide rises and falls, a naked man can be seen lying on a wet mattress that is about to sink.

Lines of white crest surge upon the deep sea; it is ink blue, verging on black. The sky is so bright and the sea wind is so strong.

The flat sea suddenly stands upright. In the trough of the waves, on the mattress about to be engulfed, the naked man, wearing only a narrow leather tie around his neck, is seen removing the black hat from his face with one hand and his sunglasses with the other. In that instant, when the tide crashes down, those dead-fish eyes and the frozen, ambiguous smile on his face can be seen.

Seen through the window, facing the sun, in the distance, on the desolate beach, there seems to be a man sitting in a deck chair, his back to the sea, with a towel draped over him. With one hand he pushes aside the hat over his face and with the other he retrieves a book from the sand and starts reading it.

TRANSLATOR'S NOTE

Gao Xingjian's fiction, plays, and critical essays on literature began to appear in literary magazines for the first time in China during the early 1980s. His book *Xiandai xiaoshuo jiqiao chutan* (*Preliminary Explorations on the Art of Modern Fiction*, 1981) created a sensation in the Chinese literary world but was banned upon being reprinted in 1982. Arguably, the 1980s were much more liberal than the Cultural Revolution (1966–1976), during which time Gao had burned all his manuscripts, diaries, and notes rather than allow them to be found and used as life-threatening evidence against him. Nonetheless, even while conscientiously exercising self-censorship, he found that his writings still caused him to be denounced for promoting the decadent modernism of Western capitalist literature. In December 1987, when the opportunity arose, he left

China for Europe. Some months later he settled in Paris, where he has lived since.

Gao himself has selected the six stories of this English-language version of *Buying a Fishing Rod for My Grandfather*: it is his view that these stories are best able to represent what he is striving to achieve in his fiction. The stories, "The Temple," "In the Park," "The Accident," "Cramp," and "Buying a Fishing Rod for My Grandfather," written in Beijing between 1983 and 1986, were first published in various literary magazines in China. These five stories are included in Gao's seventeen-story collection, *Gei wo laoye mai yugan* (*Buying a Fishing Rod for My Grandfather*), which he compiled a few weeks prior to his departure from China. This collection suffered the fate of being rejected by all the major publishers in China but was eventually published in Taiwan in 1989. The last of the stories, "In an Instant," written in Paris in October 1990, was first published in Stockholm in the Chinese literary magazine *Jintian* (*Today*) and then included in Gao's *Zhoumo sichongzou* (*Weekend Quartet*), published in Hong Kong in 1996.

While still in Beijing Gao wrote a brief postscript for his seventeen-story collection, *Buying a Fishing Rod for My Grandfather,* in which he warns readers that his fiction does not set out to tell a story. There is no plot, as found in most fiction, and anything of interest to be found in it is inherent in the language itself. More explicit is his proposal that the linguistic art of fiction is "the actualization of language and not the imitation of reality in writing," and that its power to fascinate lies in the fact that, even while employing language, it is able to evoke authentic feelings in the reader. The stories of *Buying a Fishing Rod for My Grandfather* and the novels *Lingshan* (1990; translated as *Soul Mountain*, 2000) and *Yige ren de shengjing* (1999; translated as *One Man's Bible*, 2002) document the scope of Gao's unique and continuing experimentation in the genre.

Mabel Lee
UNIVERSITY OF SYDNEY

"The Temple" was first published in Chinese as "*Yuan en si*" in *Haiyan* 7 (Dalian, 1983). First collected in Gao Xingjian, *Gei wo laoye mai yugan* (Taipei: Lianhe Literature Publishing House, 1989). First published in English in *The New Yorker* (February 17 and 24, 2003).

"In the Park" was first published in Chinese as "*Gongyuan li*" in *Nanfang wenxue* 4 (Guangzhou, 1985). First collected in Gao Xingjian, *Gei wo laoye mai yugan* (Taipei: Lianhe Literature Publishing House, 1989). First published in English in *The Kenyon Review* 26, no. 1 (winter 2004).

"Cramp" was first published in Chinese as "*Choujin*" in *Xiaoshuo zhoubao* 1 (Beijing, 1985). First collected in Gao Xingjian, *Gei wo laoye mai yugan* (Taipei: Lianhe Literature Publishing House, 1989).

"The Accident" was first published in Chinese as "*Chehuo*" in *Fujian wenxue* 5 (Fuzhou, 1985). First collected in Gao Xingjian, *Gei wo laoye mai yugan* (Taipei: Lianhe Literature Publishing House, 1989). First published in English in *The New Yorker* (June 2, 2003).

"Buying a Fishing Rod for My Grandfather" was first published in Chinese as "*Gei wo laoye mai yugan*" in *Renmin wenxue* 9 (Beijing, 1986). First collected in Gao Xingjian, *Gei wo laoye mai yugan* (Taipei: Lianhe Literature Publishing House, 1989). First published in English in *Grand Street* 72 (fall 2003).

"In an Instant" was first published in Chinese as "*Shunjian*" in *Jintian* 1 (Stockholm, 1991), and first collected in *Zhoumo sichongzou* (Hong Kong: New Century Publishing House, 1996).